A Place to Stay:
The Cornish Bypass

A place to stay:
The Cornish Bypass

by

Myrna Combellack

First published in 2007 by:
Cornish Fiction

ISBN: 0-9541918-4-6
978-0-9541918-4-9

Printed and bound in Great Britain by:
ProPrint
13 The Metro Centre
Welbeck Way
Peterborough
PE2 7UH

Cover drawing by Rob Wheeler

To the traffic

The bird would cease and be as other birds
But that he knows in singing not to sing.
The question that he frames in all but words
Is what to make of a diminished thing.

Robert Frost:
The Oven Bird

Chapter One

Did He smile His work to see?
Did He who made the Lamb make thee?

Blake: The Tyger

Friday August the twenty-sixth

In late summer, when the rain is soft and dense and falls slantwise, kids still collect in the battered Treviddick Buffet at the railway station in Camwul, where they drink dark brown tea and roll up something nasty to smoke. Behind the steamed-up windows, they have a laugh or two at a late tourist who struggles off the Riviera train, suitcase first; or pressing against the grimy glass, they grin and fawn at a returning soldier who jingles money in his pocket and forgetting where he is, stands in the road and whistles for a taxi. One year, Bermuda shorts were all the rage and no kid could be seen in jeans or any kind of trousers; another year, they all had rubber spikes on their trainers. You couldn't say they were good kids. They sized people up, just to see whether they could sell them anything, or rob them in a darker corner of Stippy Stappy or Docks Ope. The people of Camwul grumbled about the dangerous, rowdy, lethal kids. They always grumbled; yet the Camwul Echo was still printing stories about oh what a lovely place to live and how there were so much worse things happening up the line, including bombings, so don't even think about leaving Camwul now. Just hang about

3

and you'll be lapping up the Euro-money, somehow, sometime.

On such a day, a late middle aged man stepped down from a carriage and paused. When the long train pulled out, he could still be seen, just standing still on the platform. His face was raised to the rain. He had no raincoat, no newspaper, just a leather case, strapped up tight, that seemed to have been put aside empty under many others, so that the whole effect was one of collapse and vacancy; and one by one the kids turned to peer across the lines, and fell silent, sensing an event.

Kids know nothing of fashion in suits for middle aged men, but the discerning woman who stood behind the tea urn and the tea cakes, if she had thought about it, which she did not, might have recognised that it was a sharp, properly tailored Italian suit of good quality, about ten years out of date; the shirt, the tie immaculate, having the same dated style. Not that to be out of date, whether in cakes or suits, was unusual in this town, where charity shops usually replaced new businesses within eighteen months of their opening, and bread vans were always parked up in lanes with something stale for sale. But this man's shoes too, were strangely sharp, strangely new and well polished and yet strangely dated. And he himself, though he was too broad at the shoulders and chest and waist for that Italian suit with the unfashionably high shoulder pads, seemed to have shrunk inside it, about the rump and the legs.

At last, the man moved towards the flaky brown and cream painted passenger bridge. He could be seen to pause before attempting the heavy wooden, roughly felted steps and passing out of sight.

Afterwards, Annie Cole, behind the Buffet counter, said that there was definitely something about him that froze the kids and stopped them from getting up automatically to accost this man as he crossed the rusted tracks in the long since derelict broccoli truck yard, rich in its green grasses and its yellow ragwort, to make his way, a curiously bent figure in a harsh and burnt-out landscape, over the stiles and the Roadway Fields towards the winking television mast of Carn Keen and the sacred ground known as the Playing Place.

After the London train had gone, the granite mining town, now on the dole, heard the town clock chime three and drifted away to sleep for the afternoon. The kids moved off up to Tregeagle Park, where they uprooted a bench and carried it all the way down to Fish Cross. They sat on the back of it for a while before heaving it into a hedge on a bend in the steep, narrow hill-road to Carn Keen.

They watched from behind the rockpile known as Carregion Dhu, as a car-load of pensioners from the bowling club parked clumsily on the road, pushed and pulled the bench to and fro, gave up and drove on into town.   Just as it was getting cold and the kids were thinking about picking their way back through the heather roots and prickly gorse around the hillside, they saw a police car arrive.   Then they saw a Keen council lorry arrive.   Then they got bored and went back up to Consols, to some derelict mine buildings, after trying to set a gorse fire that was too wet to catch properly or even to frighten the adders, but just sort of brooded and smoked and smouldered in the twilight. It was a long time before they heard the fire engine from the great Heritage Engine House where they sat drinking themselves silly on White Lightening.

* * *

In the afternoon sun, the great house of Carlyon sat snoozing and thinking of not very much. It seemed to be taking advantage of a break in the cloud to glare down at the parkland and the people who wandered about in it, its grey roof slates and tall windows glistening and shining in the rare golden sunlight. On the cold chimney pots and in the trees, a few rooks stood about, their broods gone and their job done for the summer.

Conscious of time passing, the agent glanced at his watch and left his office in the coach house. The weather was settled and reasonably fine at last. Under his arm were some of the wooden signs he had made to put on the gates to direct the traffic coming to little John Gwarior's birthday party. He carried his posts and string carefully, intending to direct the cars himself, at the crucial moments. He certainly did not want the mummies parking on the grass, like they did last year. Last year, cars were bogged down, skidding and sliding, gouging the lawn. Last year, he was unable to leave until well past eight o'clock in the evening, what with the RAC breakdown vehicles arriving at all hours to remove the vehicles which had burnt-out clutches.

This was quite an interesting estate, though he did not feel that he was able to get on the inside of the job of managing it, somehow. The head gardener, Mr Bodruggan, seemed to run everything, and he found himself just sort of running around, doing odd jobs, such as fixing a boiler and calling in the plumbers to fix bathroom taps. Lately, he found himself drawing up plans to convert some barns into holiday accommodation, though he was certainly no drawing office Charlie, and when the contractor saw his work, he did not doubt that it would all have to be re-drawn. Mr Gwarior himself sometimes said that he was hard pressed to keep his agent busy.

Mr Cruise liked to be busy. He did not feel that he was earning his generous salary unless he was kept busy. In contrast to the estate workers, whose pay packets were quite pitiful, he felt very well off here. He had his army pension and Judith had her salary at the primary school, in addition to what he earned here. Then, of course, there was the west lodge, which they were able to inhabit, rent free. Mr Gwarior had been most generous in saying that any amount of money could be spent on trying to cure the damp. Most generous. Not that they had got on top of it yet, but there were always new treatments to be tried. Apparently, the trouble had begun when the well head had been removed from the kitchen in the nineteen twenties. Water had been bubbling up under the slates ever since.

Coming under the medieval granite archway, he saw a tradesman's van with the words Drains and Launders painted on the side panels, discreetly parked in the courtyard at the back of the house.

The agent looked up at the bottle green painted guttering and down at the drains.

"What is that man doing here all the time? It's not five minutes since he was here the last time." Puzzled, he went to investigate. "I don't know about any blocked drains. All jobs are supposed to go through the estate office. What is going on? He is supposed to collect a security badge from me."

He tried to look into the back of the van by peering through the front windscreen, but the back was partitioned off, to conceal precious tools, he supposed. He went through one of the back doors, where little John's Spaniel was busy gnawing at a pair of ancient gardening clogs.

Mr Cruise opened a cellar door and called out. Hearing nothing, he ventured a little way in as far as the arched room where the family train set was still kept under dust sheets. He hated the cellars, but went down the narrow stone passage a little further, still calling.

* * *

Having finished blowing up the balloons, Nanny strode down the corridor and through the green baize door to Mrs Sawle to ask about putting out some wine for the parents.

"Oh all right, Nanny, but I haven't time for all this."

Reluctantly, Mrs Sawle wiped her hands on her pinny and agreed to go and look at the drinks cabinet in the dining room.

"As you see, there is nothing suitable for the parents, Mrs Sawle. There are some bottles of fine wine, and that is all."

"Yes, I see what you mean." Mrs Sawle agreed that Mr Gwarior would not wish to have fine wines served to these parents.

Nanny Sarah said, "What we need is a light wine, chilled, a Chardonnay perhaps, perhaps a sparkling wine for the afternoon. What about a Cabernet Sauvignon for the red wine? This is Chateau bottled claret in the cabinet here."

Mrs Sawle did not like the idea of going down into the cellars. It gave her the creeps down there. Sometimes you could hear noises when you went down at lock-up time. She was very busy. She had just made all the sandwiches as well as the French Fancies and Fairy Cakes and was hoping to be able to sit down and see the news on the television in the housekeeper's sitting room. That was the best part of the day. But Nanny assured her that it would be disastrous to leave out quite the wrong wine, and fetched a torch from the charger in the cupboard before Mrs Sawle could say another word.

Nanny Sarah and Mrs Sawle clack-clacked down the narrow stone steps and through the medieval passages to the wine cellars, determined to find a dozen or so more ordinary bottles of wine for John's party. Instead, they found Bodruggan and Mr Drains and Launders. It was a shock. To their surprise, Nanny's torch revealed Bodruggan wearing a helmet with a miner's lamp connected by a heavy black cable to a powerful battery pack at his back. He was in wet Wellington boots. His overalls were covered in slime and ochre. The other man, a complete stranger, was standing behind him in the shadows, in spotless white overalls, looking wide-eyed and nervous. The slate flooring was wet and muddy from the tramp of feet.

"Oh Mr Bodruggan. What on earth are you doing here? You frightened the life out of me."

"What you two want down 'ere? You can't come down 'ere. Git out of 'ere, the pair of you. Women don't come down 'ere. We'm dealin' wi' drains. Drains is blocked."

Mrs Sawle was speechless, but Nanny drew herself up to her full height. "I've come down for some wine, Mr Bodruggan. The wine in the cabinet is fine wine for the house. I'd like some more ordinary wine for the parents who are coming to John's party this afternoon."

"You come to me if you want wine. You aren't suppose come down 'ere. You never come down 'ere, I'm tellin' 'ee. 'Ere. Take this. Is green wine, two year old." He handed her a dusty green bottle from a rack, begriming it with grease from his hand.

"But this is fine wine as well. Look, it's twenty years old. You must have something else. Haven't you any ordinary supermarket wine for the parents?

Somebody's been to Tesco," indicating some empty shopping bags on a rack.

"'Oo's it for?"

Mrs Sawle recovered her wits. "It's for the parents of the children who are coming to John's party. Miss Buss just told you. We can't put out fine wines for them."

"Well, they went knaw the difference then, will 'em? Come on, you two: out the cellar. Mr Launder will carry a dozen bottles up for 'ee. Don't come down 'ere again." He scooped up more dusty, begrimed green bottles. "Clean 'm off first, mind."

At the top of the cellar stairs, they all met Henry and the agent, who had wandered about for a while and had come up into a different part of the house. The agent was just asking Henry what was happening about drains, since there was a van outside. The women started immediately to complain to Henry that this wine would not do for John's party. Their chattering filled the air.

Mr Cruise was worried about the security of the house, since Mr Launder had not checked in with anybody at the estate office, and was about to say something when, to his great surprise, Henry said, "Mr Bodruggan is in charge of the cellars. If you want to fill up the chill cabinet, ask Mr Bodruggan. Don't go down to the cellars. Mr Bodruggan will do it."

Bodruggan went off muttering about interfering women to Mr Launder, who had still said not a word.

* * *

The sun was in its decline as the children came pouring out of the estate cars into the front hall. The tops of the specimen trees swayed about in the park, and all was well at Carlyon.

Christice Gwarior did not come down to her son's little party. She heard the cheering and stamping when Merlin the Magician arrived in his cloak and she heard a distant sea of chatter when the children were served on the long trestle tables. Later, she heard the fractious carryings-on of the children and the plummy squawks of the dreadful mothers. After a final slamming of car doors, the house went quiet again.

John came up, a little flushed, to tell her that it had all gone well enough, though the Bays boys had been particularly obnoxious; Nanny Sarah cleared up some sick in the cloakroom and went off duty ten minutes early to telephone her parents. Nanny was in her room at the moment, and her door was shut quite firmly. Daddy had looked in briefly, but was called away to a far corner of the estate to talk about the pheasant hatchery, so he missed Merlin and the Punch and Judy show, all of which was good, except that everybody at the party had seen them before, at other people's parties. And wasn't there any other entertainment that they could hire next year? Everybody hated the Crock of Gold treasure hunt again.

Christice barely made a reply, though the thought came to her that, well, the trouble with Cornwall was that there were very few children's magicians and very few Punch and Judy shows; and any other sort of show was unheard of, so of course every child's party was the same as every other child's party on the prep school circuit.

Aloud, she said, "And did you check that everyone was able to leave with a party bag? And did you say thank you to everyone for coming to your party?"

She thought, perhaps it was time to stop having these wretched parties at Carlyon. After all, the boy was growing up; he had made a balls of prep school and she had very little energy for those sorts of capers, but it did keep the godawful Nanny busy.

"Sarah had to make up twice the number of party bags because the mothers always take extra ones. She said she was up at dawn sorting out bite-size Mars Bars and Twixes..."

"John!"

"Anyway, they do take extra party bags for themselves, Mummy. You know they do."

"Well they... do all that driving about..." Up and down, round and round... The Brownies, the Scouts, the Sea Scouts, the School Cricket, the Choir... The wretched Cathedral Choir... Christice lost interest in the matter and turned away to the window. The boy was sitting on her dressing table stool, kicking at one of the legs with the heel of his smart lace-up shoe, putting black scuff marks on the white paint work. She wished that he would just go away now, go outside, though she loved him to bits, of course, loved him to absolute pieces.

"Anyway, Mummy, now that I'm not going up to Eton College in September after all, daddy said I might be going to school down here, so can't I have my birthday party in October next year, on my birthday?"

"You could, but then all the other children will be away at school, so there won't be anybody to come to the party."

"Oh, so that's why all the parties are held in August."

"Yes."

"I thought everybody was born in August except me."

"Well, some of them might be, John, but August is the time for the birthday parties because everybody is down and so everybody can attend. It's the tradition. The way things are done."

"Oh. But if I'm to go to school down here, won't I get to know other people who might like to come to my party?"

"Are you going to change out of your smart clothes now? Into your scruffy mufti?"

"I'm going out, if that's what you mean, Mummy." He glared at her.

"Now what did I say?"

After an interval of a few minutes, she could see him out of the window in his smart party clothes, tearing up the lawn, on his dirt-tracker bike.

Where was that wretched Sarah? The house was quiet again, now that the ghastly children's party was over, so she sidled out of the bedroom, on to the creaking landing above the dark, wide stairs. Christice floated past the portraits down to the hallway, muttering that there was not one Carlyon portrait amongst them, down the dark passage, through what used to be the green baize door and what was now a sort of godawful ugly fire door.

Nobody about. In the chilly kitchen, drawing her housecoat around her, she pulled out the bench and sat for a moment at a long, scrubbed preparation table. She looked at the empty black meathooks above, and at the nearly empty dressers. Her gaze fell upon Nanny Sarah's notice board, which had been nailed up beside Nanny Sarah's small table, on which Nanny Sarah kept her small kitchen diary and her pencils and Blu-Tack. There on the desk was Nanny Sarah's blue party folder: the one in which she kept all her instructions for running a boy's party. And there, on Nanny Sarah's notice board was... Christice heaved herself up and waddled over to it... yes, sure enough, a blinking timetable for the running of the birthday party: ending with, Departure of Cars, 4.50pm. How flaming well organised.

After coming upon an opened bottle of wine which had been put out for the parents, which was actually jolly surprisingly good, Christice tottered past Nanny's room, where she overheard a lot of muttering about that twenty pound note which, yes, Christice had indeed snaffled from the hundred pounds which Henry had put hurriedly on to the table for Nanny to buy party poppers and balloons. Well, at the time, Christice actually needed Nanny to buy a bottle of brandy to bottle the plums and a bottle of gin to bottle the sloes. So there was no need for such a fuss. Was there?

Christice felt some aches and pains in her shoulders and knees, so she could do very little more today but slip off her clothes and get back into bed.

* * *

Robert Morley Jones stared out of the back kitchen window of his modern vicarage in Playing Place Parc. He wondered whether the children's cat was out murdering songbirds, this afternoon. Oh, there it was, digging up the roots of the vine. He hoped that wasn't an omen. There was no sign of his wife and children. They had gone out for the day, so shaken were they by the latest break-in. This time, the thieves did not get the collection nor the cash-box nor the general charity box nor the blind-box nor anything else except, for some reason, a cassock and a letter-opener from HMS Cornwall that were lying about in his study. He had begun leaving the parish safe wide open, after last month's break-in, to make a point, and he had removed the parish records to the Records Office in Truro. There was no knowing the mind of thieves.

Moodily, he looked up at the old vicarage roofs and the line of trees where the rooks were rasping and squabbling with each-other. The old vicarage was, of course, where he ought to be living: there, beside the Playing Place, at the ancient centre of the parish, with the Finger of St. Coen, the ancient longstone from which all of the parish spirituality radiated, in view. He was not a vain man, but only a Rector in a Rectory with rooks around it had half a chance of being respected around here. A vicar of several scattered, battered churches had not a chance of rising above being called Dracula by the youth amongst whom he had to live. His cold chimneys, cold because they were fake chimneys, the whole estate having been fitted out with electric storage radiators, were the same size as those of the common herd; and that, he felt, made a great psychological difference as to whether the clergy was respected or not. There wasn't even a Methodist living in the Methodist Manse anymore, let alone a Methodist minister: here, in what had once been the very hotbed of Wesleyism.

It was all to do with order in society: a sense of hierarchy and knowing where people belonged in it. Ever since Mrs Thatcher had declared there was no society, only individuals, morals had started to decline rapidly. You could see it around here, with the last mine about to close, and all of the miners being put out of work, spending their money in the pubs; night-clubs opening up everywhere in Camwul. People coming home drunk, making a noise at night; even here, on the estate, where he had been assured that there would be lots of nice, elderly, retired people from up-country.

He'd never been completely at home here, though it wasn't a matter of his necessarily harbouring a longing for Wales, not like some people thought. He knew that some of the church wardens felt that his appointment was a mistake. He'd heard one of them say so, long ago, when he first came here. Some of his sermons were long, yes, but he did, usually, stick to the point, and he made a good job of a funeral. He knew that he was already preaching to the converted: that was the whole point of the Church of England, wasn't it? What was he supposed to do? Should he be knocking on doors, like those New Syncretism ladies?

No. There was no point in talking to the bishop. He would try to stick it out here, at least until his boys were at university. They had the clergy scholarship at St Michael's prep school, and he was a governor there, so he always knew what was going on, and could influence things, a little. But he wouldn't stay here much beyond a few more years. He might look to move on.

Then again, it wasn't a bad parish, not really. It was worse up the line, as they called it here. Much worse. Beyond the Tamar, there were inner-city parishes where he really didn't know how a rector coped. That was worse than missionary work: much worse, in fact. Preaching to savages on the other side of the world at least lent some urgency to the mission and some novelty to the listeners. Smuggling Bibles in to Formosa in the heady days seemed exciting and moreover, worthwhile. What were you supposed to do now, in a post-Christian environment, where there was terrible unemployment and a yawning gap between the haves and the have-nots? Where the people who had broken in here again, thought the rector was a man with money. Dear me, he was only a poorly paid social worker, in a world where trained, professional social workers were being laid off and made redundant, and were taking their own problems to the church.

This was why he said to Rita, who was getting more and more hysterical, "Take the children out to that new garden paradise attraction, on the new road, before going up to Carlyon for John's party. See how they're getting on with the building work. It won't take you half an hour to get there. I'll clean up the glass and wait for the forensic gentleman to come. It'll be nice to see him. We're getting to know him quite well, now. Myself, I shall have to stay here to greet the Gorseth committee and the Thai Mission delegation later in the afternoon."

* * *

Margaret's shop was stinking. Kevin Chynoweth put his boot to a pile of stacked dry cakes which splayed out in a satisfying manner and fell over on the floor whilst Darren Pentire eased his fingers into the darker recesses of the lolly fridge and pulled out four blue ice poppers. They were out in the sunlight and down beside the Keen Count-House bus-stop before anybody dared to notice. Only then was there a lot of squawking behind them.

There at the bus-stop alone for a few minutes, a small plan was hatched. Sucking at the bottom of the plastic covering of his cool ice popper, staring across Chapel Road at the seven nondescript miners' cottages that make up Chapel Row, Kevin's eyes came into focus upon Old Pard's dwelling.

A lot of cars and stuff went by. The town bus to Camwul stopped briefly. The driver glared at them and then went on, leaving a poisonous cloud of fumes which made the boys get to their feet and sit inside the bus shelter, that stank worse than the road.

On Old Pard's cold chimney, a nondescript brown spotted young seagull was resting momentarily, looking all about, shuffling and calling out bird obscenities. Kevin's gaze swept over and focused on the upstairs window, and then on the downstairs window, and then all over the small patch of summer-burnt grass and snapped-off plants, and the half-open, rusting iron gate that was caught open by gravel and sweet papers and old lager cans.

"I know somewhere to go to," he said, after a while.

Darren was too cool to show interest.

Darren's mouth tasted of shit chemicals. He shook his head. He saw blue dye all over Kevin's lips and tongue. He went to chuck the other ice poppers away, but then thought, what the fuck, and started on the next. It froze up his mouth and took away all the feeling. Then the ice started on his teeth. It made him wince. Kevin started to stare at the fourth ice popper and Darren's mouth. He leaned over Darren, snatched the untouched ice popper and chucked it out into the road. He watched as the wheel of a burgundy coloured Range Rover passed over it. One half of the blue plastic tube full of ice seemed to twist up in pain and try to get away, but the tube never broke. By the time the second wheel went over it, leaving a dark stain all over the tarmac, Kevin's eyes had locked with those of a rich little prick who was sitting beside his mummy in the front seat, staring down at him, holding a Twix in two fat fingers. Now he had nothing to chuck at the Range Rover, he seized Darren's ice popper from his suffering teeth and stuffed it down Darren's trousers.

Whilst Darren was dealing with his numb privates, the brand new P38 passed on through Hellick village and out the other side, up the slope and on to the new by-pass, to the new half-built tourist attraction, and then to the children's party at Carlyon.

* * *

In the early evening light, the man crossed the ancient iron-age Round, pausing to look up at the ancient longstone called the St Coen's Finger, which stood, cemented in, in its centre. He felt its heaviness and its pressure as it leaned into the wind, seeming almost to beckon to him. Walking up to it, he pushed against it for a moment, turning his face to the twin houses, Montana and Mexico, and then to the old vicarage and the Sunday School, and to the granite grey stones of the church itself. His gaze fell upon the parish notice board, which stood officiously upright beside the great Coen stone. Slowly, he read a few words from the parish playing field committee, torn by winds, besmeared by the rains, held down by rusting drawing pins: "There has been much in the way of consumption of alcohols by the youth, and the deliberate ruination of the sandpit for the children. In addition, there has been illicit camping overnight and such like. The committee has been much disappointed after funds have been raised by the generosity of certain members of the playing field committee through selling jam and cakes and dressing up in fancy dress for the improvement of the Playing Place."

Resting the light leather suitcase on the burnt-out waste-bin which perched beside it; frowning at a dirty syringe on the trodden ground, the man changed the burden over to his left hand as he walked the last few yards towards the door of the Steam Engine public house.

It was only just six o'clock. A smell of disinfectant mixed with the lunchtime's stale tobacco deposits. All was gloomy and dark except the Pot of Gold machine winking in Rescue Services Corner. The stranger breathed in deeply, as though he was drinking in a long forgotten nectar. He trudged up to the shabby circular bar, with its tarnished brass-work and its fraying cloth stools; and looking down the long line of unfamiliar pumps, he asked for a beer, any old beer, just a beer, please, sir. He passed a ten pound note across to the young barman, who had a bright smile on his professionally set face, looked quizzically down at the new small five pound note and small coins which came back to him, turned around and sat at the first chair and small round table he came upon. Here, he seemed to shrink behind and into one of the pillars, becoming a shadow.

Lost in a reverie, going up to the bar to request a refill of his glass, he discovered that somebody had already put up a pint for him; and turning around, looking out across a sea of tables and people, another man and another raised his glass and smiled to him, and said his name; and a whisper went around the bar that Dingo was out of prison and that that man there was Dingo, over there.

Then all the people crowded around, ordering pints of ale and whisky and cigars; and Billy Williams took off his own red kerchief and stuffed it around Dingo's neck; and then he took off his own Guernsey knit-frock, which he normally wore all season on the boat for the visitors, and tied it around Dingo's shoulders, over Dingo's suit; and old Robbie Harris was sent for, to play The Rakes of Mallow and Lamorna and Abide With Me on his accordion; and the Russians went back to their ship with the girls for a crate of something powerful and forgot to return, because Russkies know how to party, but they sometimes forget where they are or what they set out to do: until Dingo was faint and carried clear off his legs by heat and music and friends and ale and whisky and admiring women.

Of all the women, it was the fifty-five year old Irene who won the day. Using all the skill she had, she cut him out of the crowd and took him home and tucked him up and told him, look, the place is yours: the ex-council house; the clean cotton sheets; the Sky television control with a new battery; the cat on the windowsill and the wedding-cake Artexed ceiling in the bedroom because Dingo, your place don't exist no more. They shot your dogs; they looted your house; they bulldozed your palace in the scrapyard and they built a by-pass over the lot of it.

So Dingo stared hard at the clean cotton sheets, though he knew it all already, knew it all. The solicitor told him in the prison. The land was taken in by the council, with their new powers, because they knowed how to do that; and a man in prison, a reptile, a cold-blooded murderer of a hinnocent young man, well, he had no rights. None they could think of. Not that he was in for murder, only VAT fraud, but that made no difference to them.

But what Irene did not know, as she took his tea back down the steep, narrow stairs, because Dingo never drank tea, since a fucking hofficer once pissed in his tea, was that Dingo was not grieving for his lost palace with the chandelier, nor for his scrapyard. He was not grieving because he was a viper who killed a man. They actually got him for the wrong crime, but what did that matter? He wasn't telling. Dingo was no longer grieving for his wife nor for his son, Wally; nor for Mrs Christice Gwarior; nor for anybody else in his past: Dingo was fretting for his money, which he changed for Krugerrands and set in concrete under the floor of the outside lavatory of the palace in the scrapyard, in case he had to go to prison; and which were now under the tarmac of that two-lane by-pass to that blinking new tourist attraction. And what could anybody ever do about that?

Chapter Two

When money's tight and is hard to get
And your horse has also ran,
When all you have is a heap of debt
A pint of plain is your only man

Flann O'Brian (At Swim Two Birds)

Friday October the twenty-first

Irene never made anything in her life, except an apron when she was down school, and that was a long time ago. She remembered that it was cut well, because the teacher never let the girls cut out their own apron; but the green gingham trim soon fell off and the straps fell off and the apron was turned into a floor cloth, shortly after being taken home to her Ma. She remembered the grey tin bucket and the slate floor and the apron in the brown, scummy water. God only knew what happened to the gingham trim cap that went with the apron, or what it was used for.

For forty years, Irene made little else, except love and five sons and a daughter who was no good. She spent her Child Allowance in the pub, and her black widow's compensation lump sum on buying the house in order to avoid putting all the money across the bar, and anyway, she liked Maggie Thatcher's policies on selling off all the council housing; then just when she started to wonder about her state pension, Dingo came out of the prison, and came down on the train to Camwul, and walked the last few miles, across the downs, across the Playing Place Round to the Steam Engine, and was carried to her place on the hill that overlooked the sea. When she could persuade him to, he sat in the porch at the back of the ex-council house where, if you cricked your neck, you could just see the harbour in Maynard's Cove, with the few remaining fishing boats on their moorings, the pilot boat and the big Customs boat buzzing around all day. The long garden was already devastated by the autumn winds, but there were some beans climbing up the bamboo sticks and there were still some big bright sunflowers surviving. He studied them for hours, turning his face to the sun, or inclining his head as they inclined theirs. Sometimes, he would even read the newspapers and the occasional book that she brought home from the library, because a prison service teacher had spotted his type of dyslexia and had taught him to read at last, with the help of special colour lenses, which he carried around with him. Sometimes in the long afternoons, she would bring him an unopened carton of lager; and she promised him a bottle of Irish malt whiskey when her ship came in. She had always liked Dingo. It wasn't his fault he was a murderer: people do funny things sometimes. She was glad he had come her way at this time in her life.

For just over a week, the magic of the big ex-council house on the hill, with its long garden, seemed to work on him. Then, he started to wander. Some nights, he would sleep out, and Irene would go looking and find him in a hedge in the morning. She would dry him out and apply more comfort to him. The more comfort she gave him, the more he seemed to wander. It wasn't to do with drink, it was restlessness. So finally, she let him come and go as he pleased. She never knew what he got up to, and was uneasy about it, but she had enough wisdom to leave him alone when all he asked for was peace, because he seemed to be a man who was haunted by something. Then somebody told her that he was fitting out an old roadman's caravan that the Irish had left down by the new by-pass when they finished there, in the spring.

Her sons, who worked on the roads, were suspicious of Dingo and grumbled, but she usually managed to keep them busy eating in the kitchen when they came to visit; and bit by bit, they came to see him as a spent gale who was never going to be any harm to them: not that he was likely to be much good to them either. But that was all right. He was Dingo; and Dingo was a living legend in the parish. With Dingo in the house, there was a noticeable lack of interference in their lives by Irene. Anyway, it was always possible that Dingo would make another fortune or find again the fortune he had lost. Everybody believed he was going to do that. If anybody could do it, Dingo could; and the parish needed that kind of man amongst them, now that mining was finished and fishing was finished and there was nothing left but to say goodbye to Coen Parish and go. But to go was the same as to stay, with the whole country in depression, England too; and if you had to get drunk all day, because there was nothing else to do, well at least the view was better here than from some bedsit in Wakefield.

But what most failed to realise was that Dingo was not the man he once had been. In Dingo, as in so many men, one man went to prison and another man emerged, after fights and scrapes and disappointments, twelve years later. Only Dingo, and to some extent Irene, Dingo's close observer, recognised that the confident and integrated scrap metal merchant of the previous decade was gone forever. Yet, Irene believed that like that apron that had gone into the wash-bucket and was pushed and pulled across the floor all those years ago until it ended in rags, Dingo only needed careful attention, quiet, careful stitching, to be saved. For Irene Mason, the attempt at saving Dingo was going to be her own salvation. Instinctively, she knew it, though such an idea never came into focus. All she needed him to do was to sit in the porch, and she would do the rest. But would he sit? No. He was grateful and ridiculously polite, but he was always up and out of the house, directly after he was fed. He said, "Thank you, madam," or "Thank you ma'm," which was ridiculous and tore at the heart of anybody who knew what a man Dingo had been before he was taken away. The fact was, Dingo was uncomfortable in houses. That was how Irene saw it. If she was lucky, he would slip into the Steam Engine near closing time, borrow a pound or two from her to have a couple of beers; and if she was even luckier, he would follow her home, usually at a respectful distance. Perhaps he never wanted to do that terrible thing which was to impose himself on her.

Anyway, after a very short time, people stopped talking about it and accepted things the way they were.

Dingo was back amongst them, and that was the main thing.

* * *

In his bleak bedroom with the burnt orange wallpaper and royal blue curtains in the attics of the Steam Engine public house, Joseph Hocking was sitting in his chair beside his bed, glaring at his faded print, 'A Hopeless Dawn,' with its weeping women and its traphatch that didn't shut flush with the floor. He never got tired of contemplating the scene in the picture: the boiling sea outside the mean cottage windows, the drying seaweed on the wall and the guttering candle on the white tablecloth. Lately, sitting here, Bramley's painting was more real to him than anything that was ever told to him. He fancied that he remembered cottages like that, with the bare floors and bare, uneven whitewashed walls. He would prefer any day to sit in his bed and do without a chair altogether, but one of the interfering caretaking women from Social Services told him that he would get pressure sores if he did. If by that they meant bed sores, he wished they would say so. He was always finding new things in the picture, depending on the way the light played on the dirt on the glass and the print behind it. Lately, he had been thinking about the burnt-out candle in the window. A long time ago, he had given up trying to work out what was in the picture that was nailed onto the wall in the picture. He used to think it was a religious picture, but lately, he fancied it was a picture of a pile of longstones. Even if you got out of your chair and hobbled up to it, you could make it out no better. In fact, it was better if you looked at it from afar.

The best was when he was sitting up in his bed at night, and the moon shone on the reflection of the picture in his convex shaving mirror. That gave it a different perspective altogether. You could see all sorts of things in there, then.

Once, a long time ago, one of the nicer interfering caretaker women told him he could get better one day and get up to the Tate Gallery in London to see the real thing. He never told her anything about the picture, but she saw him gazing at it. Well, that was a long time ago, and he doubted the real thing was as good as the picture he saw in the shaving mirror.

Very few people came to talk to him, so he was able to sit in peace, except when the women came up to badger him and try to make him have a wash. Michael had him put up here, because he wanted to change the licence back to inn status, once he got the freehold, and he was already letting the bedrooms, now and then. Of course, inn status would never happen, not while there were two hotels on the Playing Place already. There was Montana House, Valerie Carlyon's house that had been turned into an old people's home and then into a 'country hotel'. What a joke that was. And there was the even bigger joke, Mexico House, old Bonnington's widow's place, which had been turned into a restaurant when Vera Bonnington went off her head and was taken away to Camwul, but was really a knocking shop now. Anyway, the Steam Engine would never be an inn whilst the hand shakers were in control of the licences, that was sure, even though it was the oldest house in this part of the world. But then again, Michael was youngish. And Michael needed to pay for the freehold, once he got it off the brewery. It was only by luck that the brewery was over-extended at the bank in a time of rising interest rates, going bust, and pub freeholds were up for sale all over the place. Joseph had tried: for years and years he had tried to grab hold of the freehold, but the brewery always said no. Not that the pub was too successful for the brewery to want to let go. Not on paper, anyhow. He always kept the paper profits down. They would like to have got him out, but he was the third life of a three life lease, and more by luck than judgement, his grandfather had chosen long-lifers to name on the lease. Not that the old boy could have known in advance who would live and who would die in the family. There were very few three-life leases extant, and Joseph Hocking's was one of the last.

Well, he hoped Michael would get hold of the freehold. He deserved it. He didn't want strangers to get hold of the pub. If that happened, the trap hatch would have to be shut, cemented over and the real business would be finished. Although, if it was sold to Michael 'out of trade' and Michael had to go to work for somebody else, as long as the parish warehouse was full, the brewing business wasn't really needed all that much. Things could continue as usual. He'd heard of breweries being bought out, up the line, then the pubs being sold out of trade as private dwellings. It could happen here too, if it liked: as long as Michael could hold on to the pub as a private dwelling.

He smiled broadly at the picture on the wall. The traphatch was the best part of it. He wondered what was down there: what the artist had in mind when he painted the picture. It was like that in the old days, when you went visiting. People kept their table over the traphatch, and a bit of sacking or carpet over the floor, and they had a long tablecloth that reached the floorboards. They used to put Granny to sit at the table, with her chair on the traphatch. That was how he remembered it. Mining and fishing went together. Down the narrow arsehole, into the bowels of the earth. That was the way it was. That was survival.

You couldn't hear the noise from the bar up here. You couldn't get the smell. You had no idea how the business was doing, unless you had people up here. Nobody ever came up unless he went down and called them up. Well, he never made proper friends. People said he was a silent man. He never had nothin' much to say, all they years be'ind the bar and down the cellar.

But now, you could sit up 'ere an' think. If you wanted to. Which you did, now an' then.

'Course, Michael was away at the moment, over in France, loadin' up with wine and cigs. Customs never stopped him. He always paid up proper, never cheated nobody. The French business kept the shed roofs on and the window shutter hinges oiled. But as for the rest... he never had no time for drugs nor weapons.

'Course, he didn' knaw 'ow Michael would pay fer the freehol', even if he could get ut. Still... That was for another generation. Joseph was finished. They would carry'm out from 'ere. Take the planks out in the ceilin' an' lower 'im down to the bedroom below. Then through the bedroom and down to the bar. Then down through the cellar and out through the traphatch. Down to the sea. No, bugger that. No not that. Out through the bedroom window, p'raps. He'd seen that, years ago. Ambrose went out through 'is cottage window, with all the town lookin'. Carnival time. Bugger that too. P'raps 'e would go on livin' another year or two. Long as it never got painful. Which it did, when 'is legs got stiff an' 'urt 'im. That was frequent now. All that standin', years an' years be'ind the bar, listenin' to people talk rubbish, when there was nothin' to say.

* * *

Mrs Georgina Dartsby, who was new to the parish, noticed Amos Dingle. She thought him a suspicious character and wondered what he was doing, wandering about in all winds and weathers. She did not like the look of him and was pleased when she discovered from other ladies on the flower rota at St Coen's parish church that he had gone to prison for VAT fraud. What on earth was the man doing, wandering about in the graveyard?

Mrs Dartsby did not know that after nearly twelve years and three different prisons, Dingo was spending his days reorienting himself in Coen Parish. Lacking visitors, except official ones in the prison, he had mentally blocked off Coen Parish from his conscious thoughts; and now that he was here again, he found that there was so much that he had successfully forgotten.   Loss of liberty had been replaced by the overwhelming attractions of freedom. Loss of the business he had built out of scrap metal had been replaced by an almost archaeological desire to find the place where his scrapyard and his rambling, flimsily built house had been. For hours, he would stand silently on the top of Carn Keen, staring down into the mining plain, where the old monuments of mining, the engine houses, the arsenic chimneys and the remains of the stamps were fast disappearing to the heather, to collectors and to improvements.

A group of walkers, public schoolgirls, seeking their Duke of Edinburgh Gold award, tried to help him, using an Ordnance Survey map. They thought he was a cute old guy and said so, but Dingo explained to them that he had to rely on instinct and memory to see him through, because very little that went on in a landscape ever got put down on a map. Didn't they know that? They said no, they thought everything was on the two inch map. He would stand and stare until the light failed him, and then he would sleep under a hedge or in the unheated workmen's caravan by the roadside; or when the weather turned bad, he would climb Cliff Hill and turn up at Irene's back door.

Nobody interfered, because everybody knew that Dingo would find his gold.

At last, after many days of searching, Dingo seemed to give up his quest. He suddenly changed tack and could be found early in the morning, waiting for the bus to Hellick. There, he would slouch into the public library and seem to read the back numbers of the local newspapers all day. People who said that Dingo was not actually reading the microfiche, because Dingo could not read, were quite wrong. For at least ten of the past twelve years, Dingo had taken advantage of the prison's education service, and he could read well enough to enjoy *Great Expectations*, or to follow the progress of the building of the by-pass from its beginning to its end, in any newspaper. The iron-haired librarian said that he would help Dingo in any way he could, but he did not see how Dingo would ever be able to know exactly where his old outdoor lavatory had been situated, since it never featured in any sort of survey, nor was it considered any sort of monument. He couldn't understand why Dingo would want to know where the old lavatory had been situated, anyway; but the reading public is very peculiar, as all librarians know.

Mrs Georgina Dartsby, snipping at bits of greenery in the churchyard for her floral display, did not know any of that and cared less. To her, Dingo was a rather nasty-looking local who ought not to be wandering about amongst the overgrown gravestones. She wondered whether he was tagged, and was glad to get back to the safety of her bungalow in Playing Place Parc.

Dingo was not acting suspiciously, he was looking for his father's headstone, and was wondering whether it had somehow been moved, because it didn't seem to be there, any more. Nothing seemed to be in the same place any more. Even the reef out in the bay seemed to be in the wrong place.

* * *

Old Pard was taken down his front path, through his iron gate and away in one of those slow, draggy ambulances that turn up at the doors of pensioners. A bad cold and a damp bed had led to the 'flu, followed by a urinary infection that turned him silly. His sister noticed that he was "talkin' funny" and wanderin' around in 'is underpants, when she went up the road to see him, so Old Pard was taken away to the cottage hospital in Camwul because the one in Hellick was closed because it was supposed to be dangerous and unhealthy.

Before he went, he told her to make sure the front room door was locked, mind, and the porch windas was shut at the back. She made sure she did that, and took the keys home with her. She told him that she wouldn't be able to visit him, though, because Camwul was too far to go and the walk up Haemorrhage Hill was too steep, but she would see him again when he come home. She wept a lot of tears that life had to come to a' end.

Then she shut up the cottage and walked down the hill, past those silent boys in the bus-shelter, feeling like she felt when she left her daughter in the hospital all those years ago, having her baby. She went back to her own place down the lane, locked the door and stared out at the fields and the mining plain beyond, that was changing every day in front of her eyes. She saw the marsh gas chimneys. She saw the machines crawling about on the newly made garbage mountain on Copper Hill that Mr Gwarior had leased to the Council and wondered what it was all coming to. That reminded her to ring the television arial man about turning the arial around to face the other mast, since the tin cans in Copper Hill were bouncing the signal back and causing interference. She'd heard that everybody else was having it done, and that it was quite effective.

Old Pard had the time of his life in the hospital. He didn't get better too quickly, but made improvements just a little bit every day, so's the staff would be pleased with their progress. Sometimes he fretted to his friends, the orderlies, about leaving his own medals and his father's medals in the house, along with his mother's antiques and china collection and the coin collection that had been added to over the years. He worried about all his money and his house, he said.

* * *

Since they'd kicked out the bus shelter windows, it was draughty all the time. Kevin sat up on the remains of the bench with his knees up under his fleece, shivering. He'd noticed for some time now that the light that used to go on in Old Pard's bedroom at the back was no longer going on at this time of the night. The place was always in darkness.

"Yeah, I think I do know a place to go to," he said to Darren, who was rocking to and fro on the concrete floor, shivering. The autumn was coming on, and they needed somewhere to go to, if they was going to, like, survive.

Chapter Three

In this world of darkness
So let us shine,
You in your small corner
And I in mine.

Sunday school hymn

Boxing Day

On this sogging special day, when the sideways rain penetrated the bus shelter as far as the plastic bench, Kevin and Darren stood upright, staring out at the piddling greyness of it all, waiting for the rain to stop. They had both gone over their options silently and individually. They could go to town, but they had no money; they could go home, but that was unthinkable; they could, like do something, but that would be boring. They could continue to stand, staring at the traffic. They continued to stand. The whole village was one great carwash, spraying water. Even the women in slippers who normally carried their child benefit money back and forth to the post office shop, were staying at home. There were no buses because it was Christmas time.

At the moment when they were nearly defeated, two tourists with yellow faces and slitty eyes struggled off the bus from town. They stood in the bus shelter, adjusting their huge blue back-packs. Darren and Kevin were fascinated. They had some sort of big map that they'd brought out of a flat square thing, hanging from around the woman's neck.

Finally, they spoke. The woman said to Kevin, with a big smile on her round yellow face, "Dur dathys. Fatel genes?"

Kevin took a step back. Darren said, "Wha? You bein' funny or somethin'?"

The woman looked down at her phrase book, confusion replacing the broad smile. The man began to smile instead.

"We are chillout layback people."

"Thas Cornish," Darren said to Kevin. "She got a Cornish phrase book. Giss a look," he said to the woman. "Thas Cornish."

Reluctantly, the woman handed over the black and yellow book.

"Thas Cornish," Kevin said to her. "Thas a good book you got."

There was an inscrutable look between the man and the woman.

"Actually, we are looking for the Wesley memorial." The woman tried again.

"Wesley? Wesley Martin? 'Ee's dead."

"Up the Crematorium with the big chimley."

"Died years ago."

"Ashes in the rose garden."

Silence. Confusion.

The man tried this time. "Map says, it exists close to this village a chapel, a small low building called a wayside chapel built by his congregation, in memory of him, John Wesley."

Darren and Kevin made an effort, but they were defeated.

"No. Not round 'ere."

"There's a St Coen chapel, which is like a old piggery now, with no roof on, but wiv a chapel window. But is too wet to go in there. Is over th' hedge in a field."

"There's a Billy Bray chapel. I think thas the same piggery."

"Thas Big Delivery chapel, Darren."

"Great Deliverance, you tosser."

"Thas what my dad d'call it: Big Delivery Chapel. 'Ee says the parish warehouse do go under it."

"Yer dad's a tosser."

"No, Kevin, my dad should know. My dad's bin a miner."

For a moment, they all stood, side by side, staring out at the rain. Kevin dropped the Cornish phrase book on the concrete floor of the bus shelter, but nobody noticed. The woman continued to read in another book with hieroglyphics.

"Wow. Cornish people have ancient culture and traditional values. Book say, religious figures and modern relics of ancient national culture transport you to a world where you don't know if you are in a dream, reality or even history. Here is community of Celtic Twilight."

"Thas a nightclub. Celtic Twilight. Up Trora."

"I say. We should also like to see a traditional dance."

"Can you perform a traditional dance for us?" The smiles were back on the yellow faces with the slitty eyes.

Kevin looked furious, but Darren explained, "No. Cannot do. Is a secret dance. Only on Flora Day down 'Elston."

There was more silence. Then the strange man nodded, "Ha."

"In May. This is Boxin' Day now, see. Christmas time."

"Ha. Now we will go to walk around this Cornish village. Bus comes in one hour. First we make a Kodak of new Cornish friends. "

Click. Kevin and Darren were captured in the camera. Suddenly, the tourists were out of the shelter, squelching down Railway Terrace towards the new flood-plain bungalows at the bottom.

When they had been gone a long time, and the rain had become a low, misty cloud, and the yellow and black Cornish phrase book had been pulped into the corner of the bus stop shelter, Darren said to Kevin, who had once lived in Mabe, "'Ow does it go, then?"

"Wha?"

"Flora Dance. 'Ow does it go?"

"Well, iss... look. Link up with me like this. You're the woman. One two three 'op, one two three 'op, one two three 'op, one two three 'op... Then: One two three 'op, one two three 'op, one two three 'op, one two three..."

"Is that all?"

"No... then... round two three 'op, round two three 'op, round two three 'op, round two three. Now, other way, other way, round two three 'op, round two three 'op, round two three 'op, round two three. Now straighten up an' start again. Iss easy. There should be four of us."

They continued all afternoon, up and down the bus shelter, until the rain cleared up completely. People thought they were bad boys under the influence of bad medicine.

They never saw the strange couple again, though the boys were prepared with the dance. They must have walked back another way, or caught a bus somewhere else, or even settled down in one of the bungalows, as first time buyers. A lot of people done that.

It was a pity, since the boys had perfected a flora dance that was really quite special.

* * *

Since he got his new heart pills, old Joseph Hocking was feeling a heck of a lot better. He got down the stairs and down to the cellar, where he fetched himself another bottle or two. He was fed up with Michael tutting and clucking like an old woman about what in the good old days used to be put down to ullage, spillage and breakage of whisky bottles. It was the smarmy Australian barman that Michael ought to be looking at twice, not his own poor dear sick father. Joseph blamed the Hotel and Catering Industry Training Board for teaching Michael to look at the figures whilst forgetting the facts. What in God's name, for instance, was a bar stocktake? The old publicans knew who the enemy was, sure enough: Michael seemed to be working for the government. Oh well, you couldn't put an old head on young shoulders. Not yet, anyhow.

Joseph paused by the doorway to the dark stairs behind the bar, with its porthole window covered up with coloured see-through paper and thought well well, how things had changed and been mucked up since his father's time. The brewery's conservatories that kept leaking; the snug that was pulled out to become part of the extended bar... Worst of all, the back of the house that used to be a private place for card-playing and private business of the parish; that was now part of the stainless steel kitchen, bits of which he didn't recognise and couldn't understand the use of. In Mother's day, there used to be women making pasties around a wooden table with the dogs coming in from the yard and scrounging bits of gristle; then, after Mother's death they used to sell pork scratchings, which they kept behind the bar on a piece of card; a few pickled eggs. His father used to brew ale and he knew how to brew a barrel or two himself, behind the brewery's back. Now you couldn't brew without having the environmental health inspectors coming down on you. You weren't allowed to brew at all without turning the place into a chemical works. 'Course, the brewery and the government were all in it together. They'd have his lease off him if they could, but they couldn't. And Michael better watch out and borry no money from the bank, as he kept telling him. No, nor put no money back in the bank neither. Trade was all right in his day. Look at the stone he bought Michael's mother: a great rock that made everybody's eyes water. Jewellery: that was the bedrock of the business. Left to Joseph, he would rip out the plastic conservatories and put back the snug. But that could never be done. The ancient carpentry, the blackened wood panels had been ripped out and left to rot in a skip, oh years ago now. He could only stand by, helpless, because he was nearly owned by the brewery, then. Well, he made up his mind and worked and he hoped and prayed that Michael would get the Steam Engine: but what was left of it to get? Because with the old wood and the old plaster and the old slates and the old tiles went something else: the heart of the place. The old dead ones were gone, but sometimes he fancied he heard them, late at night, when the bar was shut down and the winking casino machines were off at the mains, tough, wiry little men, come back to haunt the place. Perhaps it was something to do with the Round, the Playing Place being so near, you stepped out onto it when you left the back porch. That was a strange place. You didn't like to cross it in the dark when you'd had a few. Creepy. You felt surrounded in the Place and it walked you around in circles with no way out. People used to hammer on the door after closing time, asking to be let back in, afraid to go out again. 'Course, now, they just got in their car and drove away from it as fast as they could. Funny place, but the Hockings were used to it.

Joseph winked to Hedley Culver and Frank Sampson. George Robins and his boy Derek got up from their stools in the bar and followed Joseph up the stairs. So did Derek Trefula. In silence, they trooped past the public bedrooms and climbed up to his bedroom in the attic under the skylight, where they'd get some modicum of peace. Joseph Hocking never said much; he always kept the ironic distance a publican keeps, but he still had a following: little groups of men who liked to remember things as they were, and things as they ought to be. Sometimes they played a hand or two and they remembered the struggles, the good times and the bad times in the parish. And so it was that the publican sat in his stuffed chair beside his bed with his blankets over his knees, glaring at 'A Hopeless Dawn' whilst the favoured ones sat on bentwood chairs and ruminated and remembered. It wasn't the same as it used to be in the back room, around the ancient fireplace, in the room with no windows, but it was understood that the new stainless steel kitchen was really needed, and that it was a normal thing now that old and treasured places would be ripped out and torn down. It was understood and it was felt to be only natural that they would be driven up to the attic, and they were lucky to hang on to that. So, when Michael came up to complain that Father and his cronies were drinking the profits, they had a whip-round and Michael went down again, to carry on and run the business downstairs as best he could.

As the afternoon sun came around, the men started to talk about the new by-pass. Joseph didn't say much, but he was interested to hear about it. He hadn't been able to get out to see it for himself, he was far too disabled. The two miners amongst them were saying that that was bad ground down there, that that was Dingo's old place and it was awful low-lying, above grass; that Cathedral stope was just under there and the ground was honeycombed in the bottom of that valley because that was where the old Clifford workings criss-crossed with the Arthur and Jennifer mines; and that was where a big shaft had gone in before, in the seventies, that frightened poor old Ray Collet out of his wits. Didn't nobody remember 'r notice no more? Where was the surveyers in all this? Well, obviously they wanted the by-pass built quick to take all the traffic for the new secret tourist attraction they was buildin', wadn' um? Then George said that people who knew the Irish who built the road said that the culvert that took the water from off the hill was very very small, that the hard-core wasn' packed down proper and the whole bleddy road was built cheap and there must have been a lot of back-handers paid to some bugger somewhere. And Derek said yes, thas right, because look at the size of the mini roundabout that you had to drive over, and the size of the slip road that wouldn' take a horse and cart properly, let alone they new four be fours.

Then there was silence whilst they drank a glass or two and thought about Dingo's old place, the palace in the scrapyard, how it had all been levelled and used as infill for the new road whilst Dingo was in the prison, unable to get out or do anything about it; how the parish had failed to rise up or say anything, knowing that Dingo was a murderer; Christian man and philanthropist though he was. Then thoughts turned to old inhabitants of the Playing Place, old Gruzelier and his daughter Christice; she done well for herself, but then her mother was a Carlyon anyway, so it was only right that she and her boy should end up in the big house. She was never seen in the Playing Place now. Not even in the church at Christmas, now that Dingo was back. Well, that was understandable 'nough.

Then they had a laugh about the new inhabitants of the front guest rooms in the Steam Engine: the serious-looking bearded Canadian prospectors who were there for gold, whose last stop was County Kerry and who were up on the carn every day, turning over the rocks under the television mast up on Carn Keen. Old Victor said that they ought to be looking under Dingo's shithouse, where he left his Krugerrands, 'cause that was the only pure gold in this parish, except Maurie James' ring that was stuck in the roof up Wesley, along with his arm, but they'd have to find a way of digging up the by-pass first. Then the others drew in their breath, stopped laughing and said, "What 'ee talking about, Victor?" And Victor looked at the floor and said, "On'y jokin'."

Then the mood changed, and there was talk in low tones about Dingo taking over the road workers' caravan on the new road, just to watch over his money. But the idea of getting it out of the ground was a pipe dream. It was under the tarmac for good, until the end of the world, and all the obsessing and all the planning would do nothing towards it.

Joseph Hocking looked at the wall, at the mirror over the mantle and the heavy wooden cased clock that he had liberated from their place behind the old bar before it was ripped out and he thought, well this was how he would like to go, amongst friends, hissed as a fard. 'Appy Boxin' Day, everybody, one an' all. With a deft movement, he placed the second empty bottle under his chair and pulled out another.

* * *

It was a fairly dark night, damp and windy, with no moon, when Kevin put his foot to the Snowcemed wall and lifted himself up into the back garden of Old Pard's dwelling. Darren followed smartly. Somehow, they had the common sense to keep quiet. The whole event was unpromising, and it lasted just a few minutes. All of the windows in the row of houses were dark. They took in the barred wash-house, the disused lavatory with the modern Elsan and shit bucket beside it. They saw the blank back windows of the house, the dying plants in the small garden and read poverty and depression, without comprehension. The instinct was to get back over the wall into the field, and they would have done so immediately, had they anywhere else to go. But this was the promise of somewhere to go to, and they lingered, taking it all in, as though they must not forget it. With reluctance of a kind that they did not question in themselves, Kevin and Darren retreated back over the back wall and into the field, and the boys did not speak about it to each other.

Chapter Four

Où sont tes héros aux corps d'athlètes
Où sont tes idoles mal rasées, bien habillées
Dans leurs yeux des dollars
Dans leurs sourires des diamants
Moi aussi un jour je serai beau comme un dieu
Oo Sexy Boy

Air

Tuesday February the twenty-eighth

On a lovely Spring day, when the sun shone brightly through the summer bedroom curtains, Christice woke up beside Henry.   This was an unusual event for two reasons. More often than not, Henry slept in his own bedroom; and more often than not, Henry was up and out of the house before Christice emerged from some very heavy snoozing.

Today, Henry was being most pleasant.

"Today," Henry said, after making a fuss of his wife, "is our very special day. You remember?"

"Oh yes, of course, the judges are coming today." Christice sat up.

Henry went downstairs whilst Christice luxuriated in all the fuss and attention she was getting so late in the morning.   She did not know that it was Mrs Sawle who made the pot of tea in the best breakfast teapot, who arranged the tray with Aunt Agatha's pretty silver, and

51

who went outside to snip off some nice small flowers for the tiny vase, to put on the tray.

Neither did she hear Henry say to Mrs Sawle, "Make sure, whatever you do, that you bring up mineral water only and that she is occupied with getting dressed in time to greet them with me at the front doors."

"Now you know, Christice," Henry said, pouring some tea, balancing his own cup on his knee, "that this is an important occasion for both of us. I do so want to make a good job of being High Sheriff. The judges rely on us to provide them with a good luncheon, and that we shall do. Mrs Sawle has been preparing nearly all week. She has made a wonderful game soup and has placed into the refrigerator a scrumptious summer pudding."

"Oh how lovely. What is left for me to do?"

"Oh no: you won't have to do anything in the kitchen because Mrs Rowse has come in from the village to help Mrs Sawle with the cooking. What you must do is to choose a frock to wear. I very much favour the one in cornflower blue which you bought in Exeter. It goes with your eyes. Those matching shoes show off your lovely legs wonderfully, too."

"Do you really think so, Henry?"

"The other thing is, what we shall do is... it is essential that we keep our wits about us on this occasion, so when Robartes pours the wine, we'll have some mineral water and we'll drink that instead. The judges won't notice. You know, we tend to drink a little too much, once we get started..."

"Oh Henry, I do that. I drink too much. You don't. You're very good."

"Well, we'll only have mineral water during the meal. It clears the palate, anyway. And then, when they've gone we'll have a jolly good drink together, to celebrate our success. I know it will be a success. If we're tempted by the glass of wine by our plate, we can say to ourselves, that glass of wine is not for me: it's somebody else's. Then we won't drink it. Because, you see, once we start..."

"Henry, you're so clever, and none of us will let you down."

"Ah, that brings me to..." He poured Christice another cup of weak tea. " John. Do you think that we could find something to occupy him for the late morning and early afternoon? He has a tendency to career up and down on the terrace..."

"Of course, when he has a new nanny and when he has a tutor..."

"Oh, I don't know about that. I really need a secretary to answer the telephone in my office. The work has been piling up since..."

"That girl was a bad lot. Good riddance."

"Perhaps... Anyway, it's time to make preparations now. Mrs Sawle will be up with breakfast in a moment, and then she will help you with your lovely hair."

"Gosh, I am being looked after."

"Well, it is our special day. And nothing must go wrong for us."

"It won't. Oh John. Oh there you are. Do come in, John. Daddy's here."

The males disguised a scowl with a smile.

"Hello Mummy. Is that tea?"

"I'll get another cup." Henry went downstairs to find Mrs Sawle. Things were going well, but it was essential that Mrs Sawle got a good breakfast down Christice's gullet, just in case.

"What's up with him?"

"Daddy's being lovely. Now, listen, John: today, Mummy and Daddy are entertaining the circuit judges. Daddy is High Sheriff now, and this is our big day, so darling, what would you like to do to occupy yourself today?"

Jake's big brown eyes lit up. "Actually, I was going to ask you, Mummy, might I walk to the village to buy some tuck, now that I am getting older?"

"What a lovely idea. Do walk to the village. Oh John, this is going to be a lovely day. I can feel it. Look out of Mummy's window, darling: there are cormorants on the Gaul Stones. That's always a good sign."

* * *

Henry's land agent was talking to Bodruggan, trying to make sense of what the man was trying to tell him. It was already nearly ten, and there was still a lot of weeding left to do in the main drive.

"Where did you say Shaun Mee was, this morning?"

"Gone to court today, Baily. I was there when 'a told 'ee."

"Court? Which court? What for this time? I thought Mee's compensation case was settled out of court."

"So 'tis."

"So what's he going to court for now?"

"ABH."

"Actual Bodily Harm? What's he been doing? Brawling? Where? He should be ashamed of himself. Mr Gwarior won't want that sort working here, not in his position."

"'Ee's hinnocent."

"Innocent? Why's he in court, then? Why's he not at work, which is more to the point. I need him to get the cars parked neatly. Chauffeurs will be coming slowly up the drive, and things will have to be right. Mr Gwarior is most concerned about it. There's still a lot of ragwort everywhere. The judges can't be allowed to see that."

"Hinnocent 'till proved guilty. You know that, Baily."

"If he's innocent, will he be back at lunchtime, then, Mr Bodruggan?"

"Depends."

"Robartes is serving drinks in the house today, so will you pull up the ragwort, Mr Bodruggan? By about eleven? In an hour's time?"

" I got to open the gates for them."

"Well, do what you can, Mr Bodruggan. Thank you. It's a pity ragwort is such a bright yellow colour. It can be seen very distinctly from a car window."

"'Tis the bleddy wrong time of year for bleddy ragwort, silly sod. Is daffodils 'ee c'n see. "

Bodruggan went muttering away, sloping off to the bushes, whilst the land agent leaned against the doorframe of his office in the stables. For a moment, his eyes followed the line of a long, lateral scar in the stonework which appeared to be a bullet mark. What a strange place this was, with patched up cannon ball holes in the main house and bullet holes in the stables, and with the staff constantly having time off to appear in court. And another thing: why couldn't Bodruggan call him by his own name, Mr Cruise, instead of 'Baily' this and 'Baily' that? He was a land agent, for pity's sake, not a bailiff. And who was this Tregeagle that they kept calling him behind his back?

* * *

Hetty Pengelly was lucky to have this bungalow on the High Cliffs. It was built by Mr Bridger of Bridger, Maynard and Gruzelier, and was Mr Gruzelier's bungalow itself. Of course, Mr Gruzelier was dead now. He went to live in the Old Rectory on the Round in his last years, where by strange coincidence he had lived for most of his adult life. They were a lovely family. His wife, Valerie Carlyon, was of Carlyon itself, and by another strange coincidence, little Christice married Mr Gwarior and the two families were united again through their union. Life was full of lovely coincidences like that.

Still, such coincidences weren't all that surprising, when everybody was related to nearly everybody else.

Anyway, Hetty was lucky to get this bungalow. The gable wall was cracking a bit, and it belonged to Keen Council now. Hetty understood that Mr Gruzelier got into difficulties over the Playing Place development and somehow the bungalow fell into the hands of the council, eventually. That was very good, because it meant that people like Hetty could live on the High Cliff, and the council would pay. The Cornish weren't supposed to be able to do that. These places were traditionally taken over by up-country people, who liked a view of the ocean. Hetty liked a view of the ocean, even though she was Cornish, through and through. Funny, that. But there had been a lot of over-development and they couldn't sell the new properties, so they put the Cornish in them, just for a while, until they could sell them again. Anyway, it coincided with Mrs Thatcher selling off all the council houses. Hetty's boy bought hers, but then he was made redundant from Wheel Cuckoo, he couldn't pay the mortgage, so they had to get out again. She'd done quite well out of it, really, because now she could live on the exclusive High Cliffs estate. They didn't call it an estate, but that was what it was. Pity there were no shops and no buses. Nobody had thought of that. Still, you couldn't have everything. She had a view through the picture windows. What a view. Pity the windows got salted up from all the storms. Her boy would have cleaned them regular, but he had to go to Africa to look for gold.

* * *

Scrabbling around amongst the shoe boxes at the bottom of her wardrobe, Christice finally found the blue shoes with the super heels.   They really were a very elegant pair of shoes, only a week old. This was perhaps why she suddenly remembered that behind the shoe boxes was a small bottle of vodka with a mouthful of spirit still left in it. This, she found really useful for topping up the iced spring water which Mrs Sawle kindly brought up to her whilst she was frantically wrenching her dress about. It was a lovely cornflower blue dress, but it got stuck when she tried to get it down over her bosoms and she only finally got the garment in place when she tried what Mrs Sawle suggested, which was to unzip it, step into it and pull it up. What a panic. She was so nervous.   At least the vodka cheered up the spring water, and nobody would ever know.

* * *

Hetty Pengelly, from the boxroom, could look out over the heather, down the cliff and on to the beach. There was never really a lot going on out to sea, not this time of year, she thought, but the beach in August was full of things to see, at all times of the day.

Even in February in the early morning, the surfers were out by the time she got up on to the small tallboy with her tea tray and bickies. Even late in the evening, the homos were there, up the backs, when she sat down with her teapot and Terry's chockie bickies. 'Course, she seen them through her brother Fred's binoculars which he got for birdwatching back in nineteen fifty, after the war was finished. They brought things in so close, you could hear them squealing. When she got sick of holding them, she could look through her spare pair, Stephen's old army binoculars, though they was lighter, they was not so clear. There was scratches in the lenses.

* * *

Shaun Mee left the dock, escorted by the bored policeman in the white shirt and limped up to the witness box, took the oath and answered the questions he was asked. He stood with his feet apart and his hands behind his back, soldier-like. This was the second day in court and he was spending a lot of compensation money on this defence barrister, who had turned up to the court in red socks and Shaun felt equally disgusted and offended that the judge was in a pink shirt with broad white stripes. If asked (which he was not) he would not have been able to explain why he was disgusted with the pair of them, but he was.

"Why did you hit Mr Moon with your fist?"

"'Ee was sendin' messages through 'is mates all evenin' that I was gwoin' be 'ammered after I left the club."

"So you went up to him on the dance floor."

"Yes."

"Please speak up, Mr Mee. Your voice does not carry well. You mustn't mumble. We are coming to the crux of it all. And you hit him on the right eye with your fist."

"Yes."

"Can't hear you."

"Yes."

"Perhaps you would like to tell the jury how that came about."

"I went to sort un out. This was gwoin' on fer months, followin' me round the pubs, threatenin'. 'Is mates was comin' up to me all evening, tellin' me I was gwoin' be 'it when I left the club. I was in the club on me own. I went to sort un out."

"When you say sort it out, you went to talk to him on the dance floor?"

"Yes."

"What was he doing on the dance floor, Mr Mee?"

"Dancin' on his own."

"How loud was the music, Mr Mee?"

"Normal loud."

"And where were his arms, Mr Mee?"

"Down by 'is sides. Like I said at the time. I 'it 'im."

"His arms were down by his sides and you hit him."

"Yes."

"Why, Mr Mee, did you hit him when he was dancing and his arms were down by his sides?"

"Pre-emptive strike in self-defence. 'Ee leapt towards me. I thought he was gwoin' 'it me. I was gwoin' be hammered when I got outside the club. I 'it 'im with my fist so he went down. I sorted un out. No more intimidation. Problem sorted. Then I was took to Camwul police station an' charged with ABH."

"Just a minute. More slowly. We're moving on too quickly."

There was a lot of silence whilst the judge wrote things down with a pen he kept dipping into a bottle of ink. A wicked old biddy in glasses and a green frock on the jury kept licking her lips and staring at him through narrowed eyes.

"Mr Mee, perhaps you could tell the jury what was going through your mind when you hit Mr Moon. Speak up, Mr Mee. Address your answer to the back wall behind the jury."

"Fuck off wanker, take that. Sorry, your honour, sorry, sorry, sorry."

"Yes, thankyou, Mr Mee, I think the jury got that. There has been a history between you two, hasn't there."

"Yes. He threw me through patio doors in 1983 fer…"

"The jury doesn't need to know why."

"I got a limp and I got compensation. Then I went to work up at the Big House."

"Thankyou thankyou, Mr Mee. Thankyou. That's enough. Now, turning to..."

* * *

Things were going well, up at the Big House. The Game Soup was a triumph; and on the few occasions when Christice's hand strayed towards the stem of her wine glass, Robartes moved in swiftly, with a top-up of the mineral water, which was sufficient to remind Christice of the plan not to drink the wine. She just drank lots and lots of the Jolly Fizzy water, to keep her hands busy. They had got through it all quite seamlessly, and were about to take their coffee on the terrace, where the sun was warm, but not too warm, when Mrs Sawle came to the door of the dining room and caught Henry's eye.

At that moment, Henry was overcome with a sinking feeling. Making his excuses, he left the dining room, urging the company to go on out to the terrace, where Robartes was already pouring the coffee.

Henry arrived at the front door in time to see little John getting out of a police car, saying, in a penetrating mezzo soprano voice, "Don't you dare touch me. I'll file a complaint against you, wanker. I'll sue your ass."

"Oh dear."

"Is this your son, Mr Gwarior?" The policeman spoke confidentially, and so did Henry.

"Yes. What has he...?"

"We telephoned you thirteen times, throughout the morning, in fact, but you were not answering."

"I haven't a secretary at the moment. No-one has been in the business room. We are in the middle of an important luncheon."

"Yes, I can see that, Mr Gwarior." The policeman nodded in the direction of the important cars which were parked in the driveway, where the chauffeurs were grinning and shuffling about, burning holes in the shiny leaves of the palms.

"We thought it prudent to bring him back to you," the policewoman said.

"We haven't cautioned him this time," the policeman said. "But we might have done, and we certainly will next time. We've cautioned the others who were with him."

John strode off towards the parked cars and disappeared under the stable arch, where he was heard kicking a cellar door.

"Thank you. But what has he actually...?"

"He's spent the morning with his friends in the village, rooting up and throwing down estate agents' For Sale and Sold boards."

"Throwing them down in the road and jumping on them."

"Watching the motorists negotiate around them. Very dangerous."

"We decided to bring him back to you. We haven't the manpower to cope, what with the cuts, an' all."

"I do understand. I'm very sorry. Will we have to come down to the police station? I am in the middle of a rather important luncheon."

"We can see that, Mr Gwarior."

"I should have thought, Mr Gwarior, you would be able to keep him occupied here. It's not wise to let him mix too freely in the village, not with the way things are these days, with crime and violence everywhere, amongst the young, you know."

"I'll bear that in mind. Thank you for coming. I really must get back to my luncheon party. We haven't long..."

The policeman and the policewoman got into their car and turned it around, running the gauntlet in front of the important large and expensive cars.

The policewoman said, "Shit, Frank, that's the circuit judges he's got in there. I recognise one of the drivers."

"Oo and there's a nasty scratch all along that BMW."

"That sodding boy's just done that."

"We'll be seeing more of him, before long."

The dining room had emptied of judges and their honours had settled down to coffee on the terrace. Christice had somehow got left behind and was still sitting in her place at the bottom of the table, wondering where Henry had got to, hoping that nothing had happened to little John. A rotund man with red braces had engaged her attention with small talk almost continuously throughout the meal. Christice, buoyed up by the vodka, had been absolutely charming and sparkling throughout the meal. They had talked about music quite a lot, and the dear man seemed enormously interested in her career as a composer of sacred music for the cathedral choir. She had become quite fascinated by what appeared to be three scars in the shape of tooth marks on the gentleman's face: two on the fleshy part of his bulbous nose, and another which had quite disfigured the bottom of one of his nostrils. Anyway, on everyone else's disappearance, this dear man had scraped his chair into her corner, where he now had his leg jammed against hers.

She could not remember his name, but she did remember perking up when he said, "You're not drinking any of the wines, Mrs Gwarior, do taste the claret. Well now, your husband gave us all quite a surprise when he actually turned up at the assizes..." Suddenly all the mineral water was gone, Robartes was still serving coffee on the terrace, and this very charming and very amusing man was topping up her wine glass for what could have been only the third or fourth time, saying, "There are some wonderful shows on in London at the moment. Do you ever get to London? May I call you Christice? I am Archibald, but friends call me Archie. There are some wonderful hotels in London... A cracker you were at the Hunt Ball in sixty-eight, and a cracker you are now... Henry is a lucky, lucky man..." Then he began to say how much he enjoyed the claret... All Christice could remember about the incident was assuring him that it would not take a moment to go down to the cellar and fetch another bottle, because she liked that claret too and she knew precisely where the claret was kept.

She remembered getting to the bottom of the stone steps, going along the stone passage, counting the arch ways; she remembered getting as far as the entrance to the wine cellar. Then she remembered going back up the stone steps quickly to Henry, who was standing beside the open doorway between the dining room and the terrace, looking tense. The sun was streaming down, blinding her. She had quite forgotten that anyone else was there when she called out, "Oh Henry, Henry, the way into the wine cellar is blocked by what appears to be hundreds and hundreds of boxes of cigarette cartons."

Then she remembered a movement in front of her, coming from her left side, after which she was sitting in a puddle on the dining room floor: but not on the Isfahan carpet, only on the wooden boards.

* * *

At the bus-stop, Kevin and Darren watched a white transit van pull up at the red phone box. A lot of tired, swarthy faces looked out of the two steamed-up windows at the back. There was a lot of gabbling. Whilst the driver went into the Admiral Maynard to ask directions, two of the men slipped out shiftily and took a leak behind the phone box, against the pub wall. Then a woman in a dark headscarf got in the phone box and squatted down.

Kevin and Darren looked the other way.

Then the van driver drove all around the village, round and round, looking up lanes and reversing out.

Finally, the white van stopped again beside Kevin and Darren. The driver asked them the way to Halt Farm.

The boys told him that it was up Biscoe way, but it was a lie. The farm was down Treaddle. It was owned by some foreigners, and Kevin and Darren had been thrown off at gunpoint, several days before, when they went across the fields to ask for work, daffodil picking. There was plenty of daffodils in the fields and they would all soon be rottin' away, so Kevin and Darren couldn't understand why they didn' need no workers.

* * *

When Shaun Mee was declared Not Guilty and free to go, he gathered his friends and supporters around him and strode down the hill, laughing all the way, to get the four o'clock bus back to the village. But then he thought, well, hell, the day is nearly over and Baily w'nt want us back at the big house at this time of day, so he might as well, while he was in town, have a pint or two in the Forty Legs with everybody else, just to celebrate his hinnocence and good sense for smacking Rob Moon in the face and eyes, this time last year. But first, since they had plenty of time before the last bus went, they could tank up in the Crow Bar and the Seven Bells, before moving on to the Forty Legs.

It was by sheer unlucky chance that Rob Moon's friends and supporters were approaching the Forty Legs from the opposite direction of town, having had a few drinks in the Wine Bar and the Seven Stars to cheer themselves up after witnessing the worst miscarriage of justice that had ever taken place up the hill; and it was very unfortunate that both groups attempted to go in at the same narrow door concurrently.

This precipitated an incident which engaged the combined forces of the emergency services for some hours and created a legend in the town.

* * *

Old Pard was back at his sister's place because they wouldn't let him go back alone to his damp cottage, when Darren and Kevin slipped over the wall on another rainy night in February. This time, they moved up the garden and stood by the back door. From here, no windows looked over you, only the stumps of diseased old elms.

Kevin did not even try the back door, but got the windows of the porch open somehow. It took a long time, but he got there. He got up on the sill and opened the main porch window. Then he got inside.

His feet made small sticking noises as he crept across the worn and torn canvas of the porch. He looked up and saw a blackened, smeachy paraffin stove on a shelf. He smelt the smell of a Primus stove, with its remains of paraffin and violet coloured meths in a bottle beside it. He saw, but did not touch the grubby implement that was used to prick out the jets.

His child's instinct was to run very fast, very far; but he held on to his breath as Darren came in through the window behind him. Though they knew there was no-one in the house, still the boys could not speak. Kevin's chest felt ready to burst when he realised that he had not been breathing.

Darren pulled aside a felted army blanket that served for a curtain where the back door of the old house used to be, before the porch was built in the nineteen fifties. The faint sliding sound of metal casters on a metal curtain track brought the boys to life again. They paused. Nothing stirred in the dusty darkness. Gradually they realised they were being looked at by a lot of dead people in gloomy photographs. And themselves, in a big old mirror.

They looked small and alone, but they were home and dry. In their separate dreams, they saw themselves eating ice poppers and even creamy lollies, sitting on the wooden bentwood chairs in the kitchen, leaning with their elbows on the kitchen table, chucking the long plastic tubes of empty ice poppers into the firebox of the Rayburn: a hot Rayburn full of coal and wood, with a singing kettle on the top. Gar, that really was somewhere to go to.

* * *

Chapter Five

There are no letters in your mailbox
And there are no grapes upon your vine
And there are no chocolates in your boxes any more
And there are no diamonds in the mine.

Leonard Cohen

Sunday March the fifth

Kevin's brother took a great interest in the boys' description of Old Pard's house and went to have a look at it himself in the daylight, when the boys were occupied with his Sony games machine. He slipped in through the porch window, took in the bentwood chairs, the wooden clock from the nineteen fifties, a tasty Victorian dinner set in the glass cupboard. He went upstairs. There was a nice washstand with a jug and bowl and a nice chest of drawers, stuffed full with things. In the next bedroom, he began to see some promising goods. There was a gold clock with a globe over it. It had a gold woman wrapped around it. It had some delicate white marble and gold chain on it. He knew it was good. There was a watch under another globe. There were some locked drawers. Slipping downstairs and into the mean little passage that led to the front door, he tried the front room door and found that locked too. It was a poor house that smelt of promise. As he went back over the wall, he started to do some sums.

* * *

Dingo saw Kevin's brother slink past the gate of Irene's ex-council house. He wondered where he had been. He'd obviously climbed the hill out of Hellick; he had that weary, red look that you got when you had just walked up the hill. He didn't think much of Kevin's brother, he looked too shifty. Dingo wouldn't have employed him in the scrap yard, which he didn't have any more, but if he still did, he wouldn't. Kevin's brother didn't have the shoulders and chest of a man who worked.

Dingo had taken up *Great Expectations* again. He had a special fondness for the book, since he had learned it in the prison, discussed it and wrote essays on it for his GCSE in English. It was an achievement to be able to read, and Dingo had mastered reading. Most prisoners liked to discuss the convict Magwich, but Dingo liked to think about other things in the book. Now, he liked to go over the book again. It contained a lot of interesting ideas. The idea of making money abroad, in a foreign country, for instance, when everything had gone wrong. As with Magwich, and as with Pip and Herbert. They all knew about the dignity of work. Not like the git from number four, who had just slunk past the gate, who had obviously been up to no good, down in Hellick village. He liked to think about Magwich's forethought in adopting Pip without the boy's knowledge. That was a fine thing. That was doing something right. What a great man.

Dingo looked out of the glass porch, through the gap in the council houses opposite, down to the harbour in the distance. Irene was very good, but he liked his caravan in the trees by the new road. Some roadmen had left it there when the crews moved out with their heavy machinery. Dingo was quietly thrilled with it, and immediately set about building a compound around it, with barbed wire and wire netting. He thought he might get a big dog, if one came his way. There, he could be alone to think about his scrap yard and times long gone, and his Krugerrands lying far under the tarmac. He did not find it a lonely place. Prison had taught him the value of silence and of solitary thought.

* * *

The impassioned sermon had been delivered and the collection had been taken. The last hymn had been sung. Waiting by the churchyard wall for Henry to turn the car, Christice glanced across at the twin houses of Montana and Mexico, on the other side of the Playing Place and thought briefly of her old father, now fast asleep in the graveyard beside the remains of her dead mother. She clucked her tongue and thought my goodness, what an escape she'd had. She was lucky to have found Henry, lucky to have escaped Montana House, lucky to have escaped with Henry from that ghastly farm, Selina, where poor Henry had been losing all his money, and lucky that

Henry finally inherited Carlyon, the seat of her own ancestors, and less importantly, lately of his. She looked up at the St Coen longstone, which had been moved from Carlyon and re-erected in the Playing Place some years ago now and thought, God, what a fuss that was. What was all that about? Why did the village want that back in the centre of the round, when it was perfectly all right in the grounds of Carlyon?

"Just look at that, Mr Cruise," Christice remarked, glaring at some boys who were pushing at the Coen stone and having no effect on it. "Tell them to clear awf."

The usual crowd of hangers-on were coming back for a sherry, Henry's agent, the colonel, two of the pushy church wardens, Martin and his ghastly woman friend, little John's violin teacher... Henry was always inviting them back on Sunday mornings to drink the cellars dry. And of course, the visiting clergy: always the visiting clergy. This time, it was the African bishop in colourful robes, constantly going on about clean water.

Nanny got into the back of the car with John, so Christice and Henry hoped to be able to keep silent until they were in the house and could avoid each other whilst fussing over the coats and the drinks. All of that ended when Christice asked little John to have a peep out of the back window to see how many cars were following. When John replied that there were at least ten, including a Ford Mondeo, Christice started to groan about the increasing numbers of hangers-on coming to Carlyon. The drive home on Sundays was getting more and more like a funeral cortège. Henry replied that it was she who had made a sweeping gesture when inviting the bishop to lunch, and he asked Nanny to prevent John from glaring out of the back window as though the Volvo was a school bus.

"And stop him making monkey faces at the bishop's car."

Once the family was in the house, there was the difficulty of getting rid of the churchwardens; and thank goodness the Rector's wife decided to clear off with her brood. That still left a large number who were too rude not to disappear. Whilst Christice was being shrill and Henry was coping with the sherry, there was a brief conversation beside the cloakroom in the hall. The Commodore's wife made the mistake of speculating with Mrs Georgina Dartsby as to whether the Prince was likely to visit the Yacht Club this year.

"I do so hope he brings the Princess. Everybody loves the Princess. She is so beautiful. So elegant."

The Commodore's wife ought to have known better, because it was not long before the Major began to make remarks to the Commodore. As soon as the ladies were out of sight, the Major began to speak, to the great amusement of little John, who was busy tying his shoelace.

"Well, I don't know... the princess is like a coat hanger, whereas most of us like to see..."

"I know what you mean... you want to see a bit of weight on her. Let's say, you want the lines of a heavy cruiser, plenty of beam on her, well-built forecastle, bit of sheer, full in the scantlings and eight-inch armour plating over the main deck. And handles well, both forrard and astern at all r.p.m."

Christice spotted the gesticulations and the glances in her direction and seated the Commodore and the Major at opposite ends of the table, beside their wives.

Because the African bishop was here, they all went into lunch together, with Henry saying nothing and Mrs Sawle going pale, clucking over the tiny joint of beef and being rather obvious about boiling up a huge saucepan of potatoes and bringing in a large boat of Bisto on a tray, in order to eke out the food. Henry insisted on making the boring African bishop sit beside his wife, of course. Before long, everybody was chomping and guzzling, having nothing amusing to say at all. And Henry didn't help.

Therefore, Christice took a gulp of her wine and said, "When I was young, I did a very great deal of travelling, before I was married, that is. I loved the south, of course. All those colourful black mammies."

There was an uncomfortable silence. Henry went on eating drearily. Christice emptied her glass.

Little John whispered, "Wrong continent, Mummy."

Nanny frowned at poor little John, so Christice frowned back at her. Martin's woman friend, who should not have been there, had the nerve to start grinning openly behind a napkin.

Christice filled up her glass. "Don't you have a cousin in Rhodesia, Henry? Some little chap on a farm on his own out there amongst all the fuzzy-wuzzies?"

Henry coughed politely. "Zimbabwe, I think, Christice."

"Zimbabwe, is it? It was Rhodesia last week, Henry, when you were mentioning it. I'm sure it was Rhodesia. That's right, I remember now. You read out a letter from him and it was definitely Rhodesia amongst the fuzzies, you said."

There were no more boiled potatoes to hand around. People started eating more carrots.

Robert Morley Jones shifted in his chair and waded in. "When I look at the Round," he said, "I often think of Joseph's dream."

Everybody looked relieved but mystified.

He began to feel less convinced about it. "You know," he said, "the Playing Place. I sometimes think of Joseph's dream, where his own sheep stood upright and his brothers' sheep bowed down to his sheep." They were all looking down the table at him. "Of course, Joseph was an arrogant young man. Clearly. And rather provoking to his brothers. Well, I know there are no sheep in the Round, not now, anyway, but there might have been at one time. There probably were. So, what I mean is this. There used to be standing stones all around the Round..."

"Not in living memory," Henry said.

"No not in living memory, possibly, but ages ago there were standing stones, so the archaeologists say."

"Possibly," Christice chimed in. "Only some say that. Lots don't. Lots say it was an amphitheatre with no standing stones."

"And of course, the longstone, the St Coen stone, in the middle..."

"Is Joseph's sheep," said Bishop Paul. "I see." He smiled broadly, put his hands together and rested them in his lap.

"Well, I lived in Montana, and I don't think that there were ever any standing stones around the Round, except the Coen stone in the middle, which you Gwariors stole and were forced to have put back, through public opinion. There was, of course the remains of the bank."

Bishop Paul knitted his brows, thought a moment and then tried, "So you travelled all over America, Christice?"

"No no no," Henry intervened. "What my wife is saying is that she grew up in one of the houses that were built beside the Round. There are Mexico House and Montana House, facing each other, if you will remember. The one became a retirement home and the other became a restaurant, at least for a while. I'm not sure what purpose they serve now. The traditional view is that there was an earthen bank, left by the Romans or um..."

"Oh a bank. I was wondering... I was thinking of a Lloyds bank... But then, I thought, in Montana?"

"No, Lluyd was the archaeologist."

"The Celts built the banks, the earthen banks."

There was more silence and the sound of cutlery striking plates.

"I think we have all been talking somewhat at cross-purposes." Robert Morley Jones found that his laugh sounded as hollow as the empty sunday-school. "I should explain, Bishop, the old rectory was built on the edge of the Round, as was the church, and the twin houses...."

"You're in one of those horrid little hutches that Daddy's firm built in those swampy fields beside the round, aren't you?" Christice said.

Henry squirmed in his chair. "Let's not get on to Conservation of the Playing Place, Christice."

"Why ever not, Henry? Conservation is usually your topic. Didn't the Church fling you out into one of those ghastly little estate houses, Robert, and flog off your Rectory? I thought that was what happened. To save the heating bills, or something? I thought that's what you said when you were last here."

Henry went very red, very suddenly.

The African bishop smiled and said, "The modern Church cuts its cope according to its cloth."

Robert Morley Jones blessed the bishop silently, and thought, "The soft answer turneth away wrath."

Mr Cruise, the agent, thought, "The Church and the Round, the twin houses, the standing stones, the earthen bank, what do they mean to these people? In proximity? Juxtaposed? In the tourist leaflet? What do they signify? Why are they constantly making references to the Coen stone? It seems to be in the collective consciousness of the entire parish. I don't understand these people."

Jake thought, "What are they bloody on about now? They're all so pathetically boring. Always going on about houses and parcels of land. I shan't ever be like that, when I inherit the parish."

* * *

Chapter Six

'Up there,' he managed,
Where white is black and black is white, I won.'

Crow's Fall: Ted Hughes

Friday March the tenth

There was still a lot of work to do up in the sheds and in the potato fields, and there was the usual seasonal sickness amongst the estate workers. Kernow Task Force had sent the latest man down to the Carlyon sheds. This one was from the dockyards in Chatham, come here for an easier life, a cheaper house, no asians, a trip to the beach after work with the dogs. The men of the Carlyon estate had heard it all before. He was the cabaret, the star turn on his first cigarette break. His lighter flashed gold in the sunlight.

"Well, they'll buy anything down here," he said. "I went back up to Chatham with the van and brought down a load of second hand babies' clothes and prams and cots. I advertised them free in the Camwul Echo. The first call was before breakfast. Everything was sold by ten o'clock. I could have sold it all, ten times over. I'll do it again at Easter, only I'll buy up twice as much. The missus said it will pay for my trips back up. And look at the cars they drive."

There was a long, weary silence.

The Cornish looked out over the Gwarior fields and thought of poverty and making do, and their sister or their cousin or their neighbour's daughter buying their first old pram from the small ads in the Camwul Echo, because to survive down here, well, that was how it was. It was bad enough trying to get a room, a place to stay, where the landlord would suffer children for the duration of the new six-month tenancy agreement. There was no more council houses. They was all sold off to the tenants who could afford it and to the tenants who couldn't afford it. They was the ones who ended up in the bedsits. Next thing, the council houses on the hill, the ones with the harbour view, they would be holiday cottages, painted pink, with new plastic doors an' windas an' plastic tables in the gardens. Or retirement homes. And where would the Cornish live then? In the caraparks. There was always room there, where a bottle of gas cost a day's benefit, where in that bad winter you had to keep the oven on all night, where there was frost on the inside of the windas an' you 'ad to keep the baby beside the stove. Or that other bad winter, where, if you were unlucky, your van was turned over by the wind and turned to matchwood in the night, and you had to sleep in your car with your wife and your baby.

They used to pioneer in America and Australia and South Africa. Now they pioneered here. Except that now there was no hope, no new country, no hard rock to mine. No prospecting. No prospects.

"'Ere's trouble comin'."

Full of excitement, little John Gwarior wheeled the blue Triumph motor-bike down to where his friends, the estate gardeners and farm workers, were sitting in a hedge, swearing, reading their "*Mail*" and eating their crowst. He believed that they would, and he demanded that these men could and should do anything for him that he wanted.

Looking at the motor bike and at the smart boy from the big house who liked to be rough and call himself Jake, Shaun Mee said slowly with a sly grin, "No, Jake, we can't fix that 'ere. You go down an' see Mr Dingle, down in the caravan on the by-pass. Make sure you tell 'im 'oo you are. 'Ee'll soon fix up yer ol' bike for 'ee, 'specially if you tell 'im 'oo you are."

Immediately, the boy sped off across the fields towards the new road.   The men watched Jake's movements, so like the movements of Dingo's boy, Wally, as he ran, Shaun Mee grinning and Paul Grenville laughing all the while.

Old man Bodruggan spat and said, "Stop that. Thas makin' mischief, Shaun."

Mee laughed and said, "Goo on, then. Run after un and bring un back, then, ol' man. Tell 'im why 'ee can't go, after all."

Young Paul Grenville laughed at the thought of Bodruggan running across the fields. He prodded Shaun Mee with his sheers and said, "Yes, Shaun Mee. Cut it out. You should be ashamed of yourself. Mrs Gwarior wouldn't like that, now, would she?   Thas makin' mischief, Shaun Mee, so cut it out with these."

Mee snatched the sheers and threw them across the lane.

Bodruggan got up and plodded away from them, back to his work in the potato shed, ten minutes before it was necessary. Rattling up the conveyor, he dictated to the unsorted spuds, "'Ee's no Jake, 'ee's Master John to you buggers, any'ow."

The Kentish man fiddled with his gold lighter, looking bewildered, not understanding what was going on. Nobody told him. He continued to gabble on about his van and his cheap second-hand goods in the silence as the men turned away to their potato sacks.

At four o'clock, Bodruggan told him he was unsuitable for the work, and he was inclined to agree. These were horrible, unfriendly people. He went back to Kernow Task Force and signed up to start his own business, selling this and that.

* * *

Whilst the boys were sitting in front of Kevin's brother's new computer game in the afternoon, Kevin's brother got on with hunting for money in Old Pard's house. He started upstairs in the chest of drawers in the back bedroom. Top drawer left yielded nothing but pairs of socks, silk handkerchiefs in yellowed boxes with dusty cellophane windows, a few ties and some gold studs, which he missed. The next drawer yielded some odd tin boxes, one with an old dead king on it: the one that abdicated. He found a lot of military buttons in there, which he left alone. The next drawer down was not so easy to open. It was stuffed full with moth-eaten jumpers.

Underneath the jumpers was a collection of old pound notes and currency that was out of date. Kevin's brother hesitated in front of it before moving on. The bottom drawer was even more difficult to open. Kevin's brother had to sit on the floor to do that. When it did open, it opened unevenly and Kevin's brother tried to kick it back into closed position, where it stuck fast at an angle. He had to regain his breath before attempting to open it again. Once open, he found nothing but a tin box with out of date mining shares in it, which he left alone. He shut the drawer on them. He left the house when he felt a cold, grasping, silver-tinged shade behind him. He bounded down the stairs, through the porch window and out into the yard. It was nothing. He had just freaked himself out, that was all. He didn't want to go there any more. He would sell on the information.

* * *

A boy with brown eyes was staring at him through the wire netting. A cold wave passed through Dingo, momentary, inexplicable. They were Wally's eyes. For a moment, from the dead, he caught Wally's frown and heard his laughter. Then the illusion was over, and the boy spoke to him.

"You're Mr Dingle."

"Am I?"

"Dingo went to prison. Dingo killed one of his own drivers. In cold blood. On the sea."

"Did 'e?"

"They cleared away your house because you were a squatter and you had no rights. They shot your dogs and looted your house. Then they built the by-pass."

"Did they?"

The boy dug into his pocket and brought out a broken, oily cog. Dingo relaxed, put down his bucket. The kid was alone, but he retreated to the caravan steps anyway and sat down on the topmost rung. He had no shotgun.

"Have you got one of these? For a Triumph six fifty, nineteen sixty-nine?"

"I used to 'ave, but 'tis all gone, boy, like you said. I got no scrap yard now."

"Oh, I see." The boy looked down at this feet.

Dingo had seen that look before. Christice did that once, in his house, that night when she was thwarted.

"'Ere. You're young Gwarior."

"Yes, I am. How did you know? You've been away twelve years. Bodruggan told me. You were put away in the month I was born. I was born late, which is quite common for a first birth."

Dingo thought for a while. "Yeah, I bet you was. I bet you was. You're exactly like your mother. A proper Carlyon."

"What's it like in prison? I've been expelled from my preparatory school in Somerset." A choir-boy's smile crept over his face. "I set a fire in the basement. It made a lovely blaze. I'm not allowed to return to collect my mathematics prize. And now, my father has withdrawn my name from Eton College. It's quite a scandal. But I'd do it again if they sent me away."

Dingo frowned and looked into the trees. The pines were echoing the boy's treble voice. It was his own voice, and Wally's voice. It was a Dingle voice. "Don't go sayin' that," he said, "or they'll 'ave 'ee in prison too, before yer time. What's yer name, anyhow?"

"Jake."

"Jake Gwarior? What's yer real name?"

The boy scowled. "John. John Alfred Henry Bevill Gwarior."

"Oh dear. I see. An' where do you live, Jake?"

"Over there." He pointed in the direction of the hollow on the hillside where the great house of Carlyon lay dozing in the shade of its own history. "In the big house."

There was a long pause.

The boy picked up a stone.

"An' yer Aunt Agatha? Is she gone?"

Jake nodded. "She's dead. And her servant Gilles went to Morocco for a holiday because of his rheumatism and hasn't returned."

"An' yer Uncle Martin?"

"Martin's not dead. He's not even very elderly, really. He's not my uncle, he's my second cousin, agnate. He's only a few years younger than my father. He has dinner with us on Fridays, when I have to dress properly. He's taken early retirement from the hospital and rents the North Lodge on the estate. The lodge was designed by Edwin Lutyens, but it suffers from dry rot and has an awkward kitchen, so he spends most of the week lodging comfortably with the widow of an industrialist at the top of Carlyon Pill."

Dingo laughed at the thought.

"I'm glad my family amuse you," Jake said. "I find them very dull. Goodbye, Mr Dingle. You were my last hope of getting my Triumph on the road."

"You like bikes, do you, kid? Why's that, then? Tell you what, you wheel it over 'ere an' I don't promise nothin' but I'll 'ave a look at un, get un gwoin' fer 'ee if I can. Alright?"

"All right. All right. Thank you, Mr Dingle. I knew you would help me. I'm coming back."

"Did your mother send you?"

The boy sprinted off down the valley track, dodging the gorse and heather roots in his path.

Dingo reached into the van and opened a can of beer. He shook his head again and stared into the trees. Then he looked up at the open sky and reached with the other hand to feel his clean clothes drying on the line which he had strung between the caravan door and one of the Scots pines. He wanted to laugh with pride, because nature suddenly whispered to him that he had won the sperm race, twelve or thirteen years ago; and he found that he could not laugh. Like a dye that was spreading through his innards, Dingo was beginning to understand profoundly that this child was his own child.

At first he thought, as he sat there in the sunshine, "Well, let it go, let it go," and tried to smile with pride at the cheek of it all, that that beautiful boy had come into being, like some immense mystery forming, unknown to him, changing everything in the world, unbeknownst to him as he worked his time out in the scrapyard and in the prison.

Then, as the sun fell into the pines and the trees and the sun threw flashes of dark and light onto his face, he said, "When will she come and tell me? Does she know I'm down here? Did she send him? How will I pay for the boy? He must go to Eton College after all. He only set a small fire. Thas boys for you. Education is everythin' in 'is position. 'Ee'll have a big position in life one day. 'Ee won't go to work like ordinary people. 'Ee'll have to run Carlyon one day and be a magistrate. Will she fix me up with a job on the estate, I wonder?"

Later again, when the lager cans were empty and were stacked against the hardboard wall, the loneliest thought came and echoed around the dark place: she would never come down here, to the road men's caravan by the road, to tell him. She was never seen in the village now; and now he believed he knew why.

In the night, he wondered if it would be right and proper and decent to go and see her about it. Wasn't it his place to go and see her? He'd been in Carlyon before, with his camel hair coat and his Daimler with the white-walled tyres, incredible though it seemed now. She might see him in the muniments room in the tower, like Agatha had seen him before, when he had business there, when he was giving away Wally's dirty drugs money to the hospital. He liked to hold that thought in his mind, that she would see him in the muniments room; but it kept slipping away from him. How would he go and see her? How would he get in to see her? She was surrounded by people of her own sort. What would he say? "Now then, Christice, this 'ere boy of yourn and Henry Gwarior's, well 'ee's reely mine, idn'a? Now, you know you can't fool me, Christice. I want a proper part in his up-bringin'. I must pay a fixed amount every week. I must work and 'ee must go to his Eton College."

But Dingo had been a stupid fool. He had one chance with her, and she didn't like him. Time had gone on. The rich was richer and the poor was poorer. Lady Agatha was dead; Henry had inherited everything and Christice had gone up to Carlyon to live, as everything was predicted twelve years before. Dingo had sunk a long way since then. So, let it alone and keep it all in the dark. Then, he was back in the prison, fighting his corner, saying yes please and no thank you, sir, struggling to read a book with the tutor, because in a book was knowledge, and if he could climb high enough on this library ladder, to get this book, it would get him out and over the wall, if only.

At first light, he awoke with a start. Everything made of metal was sweating and dripping inside the caravan. Sitting up in his army blanket, he got over his first fit of coughing, cleared a window and looked out. The white seagulls on the tip were giving it welly already this morning. He crept out into the dawn, down the caravan steps and into the heather. In the sweet air, he could catch his breath. And in the heather, there was something new. A shape that glinted a bit in the morning light. At first he approached cautiously. It looked like a human being in a blanket. He hoped to God it wasn't. He didn't want no shocks like that. But then, to his joy, he saw what it was. The bike was over there, with a blanket, a travel rug half over it. The boy must have come with it later, wheeled it down, like he said he was going to, when Dingo's caravan door was shut. Why did he shut the caravan door when he could have kept it open? He went over and felt the wet handlebars, pulled it upright and sat down into the wet saddle and tried the spongy kick-start. He felt instantly what was wrong with the bike. Well, and it was no dream. The boy, Jake, had left the Triumph there in the heather, for him, his own father, to put right for him. Of course, he didn't want to bother him again, once his caravan door was shut. He was a polite boy, well brung up. He just left it there for Dingo to sort out and fix up.

And he would do it, somehow, though he didn't know what to do. He had no money, but he did have time. He had all the time in the world to do it. There were all the other scrap metal merchants in Cornwall: one time, he knew them all. Somebody would get his cog for him. They would get his bike going for him. If it could be done, it would be done. Didn't the boy say he would be back? Dingo didn't like the valuable motor bike being left out there in the wet. What a stupid man he was to leave it out there all night like that, when he'd been trusted with it. Anybody could have pinched it overnight, while he'd been sleeping off his pack of lager: and what would he say to his boy then? He didn't have no shed yet, not at the moment. He would get a shed as soon as possible: that was his next task; but until then, to be safe, the bike would have to come in the van with him.

Finding new strength, Dingo very gently eased the motor bike up into the van and wedged it down between the bench and the table. Then, lying down on the other bench, his breath coming more easily, he sat looking at it for a long time, thinking about getting a bus from the village as far as Truro, and walking the rest of the way to Combellack's Farm Shop and Car Spares, down Malpas way.

* * *

The moon was behind a bank of cloud, that night that the big man and his little wife got over the washed-out Snowcemed garden wall of Old Pard's place. It was a windy night and the old woman who slept in the cottage next door to Old Pard's place was fast asleep. So was the rest of the village. Their van was parked down the lane, waiting to go. They used the old tin trunk that Old Pard's sister had taken into service with her, nearly sixty years before; and they used the tin hat box that had transported Old Pard's mother's hats to the cottage, eighty years before. Finally, they pulled out the big old trunk that had come from Mexico a century before. The two great dinner services and the china ornaments that were wonders and were never seen nowadays, were packed carefully into the trunks, wrapped around by embroidery that Old Pard's mother's black nurse sewed in the luminous nights in

California. The golden ormolu clock that Old Pard's grandfather used to wind when he was a young man was packed away; but in the dark, they failed to see the winder, so that later, when the moon came round from behind the trees, it shone gold in the moonbeams, delicate as an old lady's protest, not that there was anybody left in the house to see it. The coin collection was put into the small trunk, and the delicate stuff was packed around with linen and with embroidery that had been done by the black nurse in Pachuca, who had nursed Old Pard's mother in Mexico, when she was a baby. They went on to crowbar the front room door, where they took most of the china in the glass cupboard, leaving much of the glassware behind, especially after a shelf yielded to the big man's foot and the colourful glass birds crashed to the floor. They took the big family bible, with the names and the dates of births and deaths, going back to the early eighteen hundreds, because it was full of illustrations and gold leaf. They took Old Pard's brother's watches and rings, which would be sorted out later. They took Old Pard's father's first world war medals. Most exciting of all, they were able to take away nearly forty thousand pounds from odd nooks and crannies in the cottage. They left the wills behind, and even the keys to the empty boxes on the kitchen table. They were fair: purposeful and fair. And they didn't damage anything. No shitting on the mats, nothing like that. Then they exited by the porch window, carried the heavy trunks down to the van and drove away into the satisfied night.

* * *

Chapter Seven

You are the one
Solid the spaces lean on, envious.
You are the baby in the barn.

Sylvia Plath: Nick and the Candlestick

Sunday March the twelfth

On the way to Malpas, walking down the narrow path beside the Keen river, Dingo started to think about his wooden fishing boat, his old crabber that had been built at Mylor. He wondered what had happened to it, with its brass binnacle and its snug cabin. Nobody mentioned it to him, so he assumed that it was gone, like everything else that belonged to him. If the boat was still there, up on the mud where he left it at the top of Carlyon Pill, perhaps he could move into it for the winter. It would beat living by the roadside. Anyway, it would be closer to the boy, in case he wanted to come down and see how the restoration of his bike was coming on.

After Old Man Combellack assured him that he had no spares for anything much these days, since everybody is mad on buying new, because to borrow money is now cheap, and he certainly had nothing for a Triumph 650, "that being a really specialist bike now, Dingo, you should know that, old son," Dingo got the bus back to Hellick and walked across country to the top of the pill. As he came down between the small, steep fields in the gloom, he paused beside a substantial thorn tree on the rocky path.

So there it was, the pill. A great forest of masts rose from the water, obscuring even the contours of the river, where, twelve years before, there had been no masts but that of Lady Agatha's solitary, wooden yacht. It had all changed; he knew, before looking further, that his boat had gone. It would not have survived this sort of change.

As he moved towards the water, a flight of egrets rose from the foreshore and started to shriek across the pill before settling to roost in an old tree leaning over the water. Well, that was another change that had taken place. He didn't remember these little white birds being here. He sat and watched them for a while in the gloom. Some good things had happened on the river, then. For a while, he stared at the dense, darkening oak woodland across the water. Scenes from the past came to mind: bright, shining days, muddling about on the boat, not knowing what to do on it, really, polishing up the brasses, enjoying the movement of the water, hearing the bird calls and wading to shore with little Wally on his shoulders at the end of the day. What really happened to Wally? His mind, unwilling to suffer more pain, shifted swiftly, automatically, sideways to another scene on the river. He wondered what that daft wanker, the Frenchman Gilles was doing with hisself these days in Morocco. He grinned, chose a piece of sweet grass beside him and chewed it for a while.

It was quite dark when Dingo got up stiffly and slid down to the muddy bank. A startled kingfisher burst out and tore ahead of him, low on the water, like a guided missile, a flash of blue and green. The river bank was a cold and damp place, but he would rather live down here, if it was at all possible. With a heavy sigh, he looked up to the top of the pill, where the grass met the mud, and saw in the gloom, as he had predicted all too well, that there was no trace of his own boat, nor of the dozen other abandoned and rotting wooden hulls that used to grace the foreshore.

He moved on up to the spot where twelve years ago, he had carefully brought his boat up with Johnny Edwards on the top of the spring tide, secured it well on the mud and grass, that final afternoon in the sunshine, telling Johnny where the keys were kept; telling him how things worked; telling him to use the boat a bit and look after it; bring the missus and the kiddies down with their sandwiches and their flask of tea; only tell them to watch out for the dangers on the river. He might not be away too long, he heard himself say. They might not keep him so long. It was only to do with VAT returns. But then, a few months and fights with his fists and failure to ask for parole or to co-operate with authority led to years inside, lightened only by the prisoners' literacy programme. What was there to come out to? His son, his house, his home, his business were all gone. He would rather not face the outside.

And then his memory wound forward to that moment of leaning on the bar in the Steam Engine, twelve years later, asking Irene's brother, "So, 'ow about ol' Johnny Edwards? I ebn seen un since I bin back."

"Johnny Edwards. Oh well, 'ee got a redundancy payment from Wheel Cuckoo. 'Ee went Florida with 'is fam'ly for a 'oliday. 'Ee ebn bin back. Nothin' doin' 'ere. No work. Lot of um done that. Jes stuck to America, long as they can."

Dingo began the long walk back to the road in the gloom. Under the trees, he stood listening to the river sounds, the old longing for a cigarette suddenly returning urgently, though he had given up tobacco in prison, using his tobacco for currency. Filling his lungs with the dank air, he moved on, picking his way over stones, pebbles and tree-roots, in the reflected light from the river.

In his widow's house on the river, Martin said a few words to Anne, drew the curtains, turned off the television news, undid the catch on the French windows and strolled out onto the lawn which ran down to the foreshore. Stepping down onto the pebbles and sand, thinking he would just check the moorings of his wooden rowing boat and have a look at the weather in the last light of the day, he saw a solitary, grey figure moving towards him. He knew who it was.

"Amos Dingle, isn't it?"

"Martin Gwarior, idn'a?

They spoke together and paused awkwardly, standing still, six feet apart.

"I heard you were out," Martin said. "I'm glad. I hope you were not treated badly."

"No, not bad," Dingo said. "Not bad. Not considerin'."

Martin gestured helplessly towards the house. "I'd invite you in but, you know how it is."

Dingo knew how it was. He saw that Martin had started to grey, and that his hair was thin. "I heard you've not been so well," he said.

"No, not so well," Martin said.

"Is they machines," Dingo said. "I told 'ee so at the time."

"Well." Martin looked up at the darkening sky. "Plenty of people suffer from testicular cancers, Amos. Not all of them are radiographers."

"Well," Dingo said. "Don't forget, I told 'ee so, at the time."

"I worked on the Linear Accelerator for years. Until it and I wore out and we were made redundant and replaced."

"You done a good job, then."

"I have always thought that it might have been you who had also done a good job, made things possible, Dingo; though how and why, I did and do not know, to this day."

Dingo looked at the ground. "Don't talk riddles, Martin. There's nobody else 'ere. We'm old men now. Our day is nearly bout over."

"All right. I think you provided the Linear Accelerator, and I don't know how or why. I think you gave the money to Aunt Agatha, all those years ago. But what I don't understand is why you donated all that money to the committee chairman to buy the Linear Accelerator, and then the next thing was, you were going to prison for failure to pay VAT."

Dingo paused. "What you say may be near," he said. "But there's a lot more to it than people might think. So, you may be right; and then again, you may be wrong. But there's one kind of money, and then there's another kind of money, an' they can't never meet."

"They say you murdered your son's friend, yet you went to prison because of failure to pay VAT. I don't understand."

There was a long pause.

"Martin," Dingo said, "All of these things was a long time ago. Wally's friend will turn up before long, and so will Wally."

Martin turned away, knowing that Dingo was a closed book; but Dingo followed a few steps. "I think, Martin, that it may be that I have another son. I want to do the right thing, do the best by un. I just can't... Perhaps you do know what I mean."

"No, I don't," Martin said. "You know, these waters are awfully deep. There is a tide-race here ..."

Martin stood on the bottom step to the lawn of the grand house by the river. A light went on in the comfortable dining room and a curtain twiched.

"Must go," Martin said. "You know how it is. Mustn't keep a lady waiting."

Dingo trudged on along the foreshore, striking inland along a narrow woodland path that would soon be overgrown with spring ferns. "I wouldn' know," Dingo said to the path, "not any more."

Martin watched Dingo merge into the dark.

"Did the old tramp want some money?" Anne asked Martin.

"No," Martin replied. "He just wanted some company. Just passing the time of day. I knew him once. He kept a scrap yard. He did well in his time. Of course, you wouldn't know it now, to look at him. He lost it all when they built the by-pass."

"What a shame."

Martin drew the heavy curtain against a darker sky. He put his heavy outdoor shoes in a cupboard and slipped on his navy-blue slippers with white piping.

* * *

Chapter Eight

Trumpet sounds within-a my soul
I ain't got long to stay here.
Steal Away

Negro Spiritual

Sunday March the nineteenth

"Jesus said, I am the real vine, and my Father is the gardener. He breaks off every branch in me that does not bear fruit, and he prunes every branch that does bear fruit, so that it will be clean and bear more fruit. You have been made clean already by the teaching I have given you. Remain united to me, and I will remain united to you. A branch cannot bear fruit by itself; it can do so only if it remains in the vine. In the same way you cannot bear fruit unless you remain in me. I am the vine, and you are the branches. Whoever remains in me, and I in him, will bear much fruit; for you can do nothing without me. Whoever does not remain in me is thrown out like a branch and dries up; such branches are gathered up and thrown into the fire, where they are burnt. If you remain in me and my words remain in you, then you will ask for anything you wish, and you shall have it. My father's glory is shown by your bearing much fruit; and in this way you become my disciples. This is the gospel of our Lord."

Dingo stood at the back of the church, listening to Mrs Georgina Dartsby enunciate the lesson. Everybody else was sitting down. The lady churchwardens were looking back at him, nodding at him fiercely to encourage him to sit, but Dingo did not feel able to do so. It was the first time that he had set foot in the church since his return to the parish, and there was only a handful of people there, all women. He didn't seem to belong to the church any more. All the pews were the same; there were the same medieval paintings on the wall; there were the same mysterious tiles and drapes and boards and artefacts; the same communion rail. But Dingo did not feel able to go up any more. He wasn't dressed for it, he felt. He wasn't shaved; wasn't tidy enough; wasn't good enough. There were plenty who would agree with that.

Somehow, he failed to take in the vicar's words. He used to like the sermons, especially when the clergy stuck to the Bible stories and didn't try to be relevant. He looked up at the roof and the old Bible that was stuck up there in the beams, where Eli Ashcroft had chucked it after the last war. He looked up at the white windows, at the last piece of blue medieval glass that somebody had forgotten to poke out in the Reformation. He checked that all the pews were there, especially the medieval pew with the Breton piper.

Yet it was not history that moved him. It was Hetty Pengelly's wobbling voice in the opening of the Collection hymn, "Fierce raged the tempest o'er the deep..."

These days, in all his daydreams, he saw Peter's young face in the moonlight, not Wally's, his own son's.

" 'Save Lord, we perish,' " was their cry.

" 'O save us in our agony!' "

In the old cadences, and in the organ's rolling of the bass line, hammed up by Butcher Bray, the weak soprano voices trilling to the rafters over and above it, his whispering conscience had finally begun to rise within him. He was damned to live with the memory of his revenge killing and damned to die with it. The church was no place for him. He wondered what kind of man he had once been. He did not recognise him now, but this man went on paying for that man's deeds.

He went out quietly. How can the Church redeem? How can the Church redeem?

He wandered about outside, down the path and into the graveyard. He saw that brambles had advanced over the headstones, even up to the locked doors of the old Sunday School. He wanted to have a look at his father's headstone, which had been erected in another time, a period of time when Dingo had a lot of money to spend on keeping his end up in the parish; a time when Dingo was not ashamed of spending money on whitewashing his father's memory. An explosive mixture of pride and sadness and embarrassment flooded through his mind, seeing in the distance the white marble angel which stood above the brambles, now greening and streaked by the weather, and his fists clenched. He was unable to reach it. There was a barrier of thorns between himself and the stone. The trouble with being in prison was that things like this were neglected, these all-important monuments. When you came out of prison and returned, you wandered about in a landscape that had been altered, and not only by man, but by the march of the seasons. Time and ideas and people had moved on, and you were left to wander about in an alien place, people nodding to you from a distance. He supposed that was how it had been for all of those solitary men who used to come back from South Africa and America: men in bright shirts with short sleeves, he saw fleetingly wandering up and down the byways when he was a boy, their deep suntans fading. They never lasted long. Before this morning, before he saw into the reality of it, he had fancied himself borrowing Irene's trowel and weeding around the curb and the gravestone; but he saw now that the task was altogether too great, and that there was no point to it. For a moment, he wondered where he belonged. He had come back here because it was all he knew. This, he had thought, was his home, not just somewhere to go to, after his release.

The Cypress avenue was still there; but the trees had grown too tall and wide, and the walk beneath was dank and overgrown, and was turning into a swamp in which their shallow roots would die. He turned away, shut the graveyard gates and went back to the church porch.

The last hymn trilled itself out. Dingo listened intently.

"So when our life is clouded 'oer,
And strong winds drift us from the shore,

Say, lest we sink to rise no more,
' Peace be still.' "

What peace was there for a man who clubbed a boy over the head and sent him to the bottom, without remorse, without even the ability to say amen? A man who had fathered another boy without even knowing it.

He could ask the rector whether he might go inside the locked Sunday School room, where the Baptismal Roll used to be kept, just to look up Wally's name again. But he was seized by a contrary thought that the white roof would be blackened green and damp by now, and that some things were best left in the memory. He thought, with great waves of sadness, how harsh he had been to the resentful Wally, trying to bring up his wild boy alone without a mother, when all he could think of doing at the time was to send the boy to Sunday School every Sunday he was home from his public school and to go to church himself and be a churchwarden; and it was all done to push back his fundamental feeling of inadequacy. As though the church ever helped anybody to push back the wickedness of bad influences. Here, he turned his mind away from the familiar track it wanted to follow.

A very new hall of some sort had been built on the side of the church. He had never noticed it before. He walked down the new cheap ochre and red patio paving blocks, and tried the door. It was unlocked. There was a small entrance hall with a few new gold coloured coat pegs. He did not hesitate to read a brass plaque on the wall. Well, that was something. That was progress: he could read the name of the third generation Cornishman from Seattle who had never seen the place, but who had had a vision that he must do something for the parish of his ancestors. He wondered who this benefactor was. A burglar? A man with a conscience? A man like him, Dingo, who once had a son who was dead and never coming back and who left behind him an embarrassing sum of money? Dingo knew all about philanthropy.

The last prayers and blessing had been mumbled. The congregation was preparing to leave the church. Dingo made the decision to wait for the rector to come in to the new building. He knew he would follow his flock. Robert Morley Jones wouldn't remember Dingo, but then again he might. Dingo would ask to see the old Sunday School for the last time, just in case they decided to pull it down, the way they did, these days.

In the interior, his way was barred by an imperious woman by the tea urn, who asked him to wait by the side door, because the congregation would be coming out very soon, and he would have to have his coffee first, before they arrived. She imposed her body, barring entry.

"Stay there," she said, and he saw, as from a distance, his real position in the parish. Mr Dingle, the churchwarden, was long dead. Now, he walked in the body of Dingo the tramp, and he must suffer Dingo the tramp's privations.

With great caution, she brought him a cracked cup of cheap instant coffee, full of sugar and very little milk. He watched her very carefully whilst she prepared it, the old prison suspicions of dark beverages rising in his throat.

The woman stood on the concrete step with her arms folded, watching him, whilst the rooks squawked and rasped in the trees. Dingo looked away and handed back the cup.

She shut the door in his face and locked it from the inside. After a while, people drifted in from the service, through the main door. The woman complained instantly about a tramp at the door who gave her back her coffee, after she had made it for him. "You can't help these people."

One or two people exchanged a glance. Gloria Tregaskis said, "What did he look like, this tramp?"

There was a silence, and then, Joseph Pengelly's wife, Mary, said, "We jes' made you a churchwarden, ebm us? You jes' come down from Guildford and you jes' bin made a churchwarden, 'ebm 'ee? Waal, you know who that man was, you was talkin' about? That was Amos Dingle, and 'ee was a churchwarden 'ere for eight year, before 'is fall. 'Ee 'ad a son called Wally, 'ee died in a boatin' accident twelve year ago. 'Ee brought 'is son 'ere every Sunday, rain or shine. They lived out on the downs. 'Ee was a rich scrap metal merchant, an' a great philanthropist to this parish."

A wind was rising. The brambles seemed to be moving about in the churchyard, clawing and scratching. The rooks had become urgent in their squabbling, fetching twigs and battening down.

"A churchwarden? You must be mistaken." The woman looked nervously at the open door, where the Easter sunlight was streaming in.

"Oh no, dear, I ebn made no mistake. That was Dingo, the philanthropist, come to prepare to celebrate the risen Christ, to 'ave a cup of righteousness with plenty of milk and no sugar outside the back door of 'is old Sunday school with the new kitchen that 'ee 'elped us to pay for."

And Robert Morley Jones came, and said, "Yes I remember Amos Dingle. Surely he was not here walking about among us? I never saw him. I never recognised him. Why was he not invited in?"

Dingo went back across the Playing Place and along the road to Irene's for Sunday dinner. He was too disheartened to enter the doors of the Steam Engine. He knew she would not be there, but would be cooking at this time of the day, whether her men turned up or not.

At the back of the wind was rain. It was quite a squall. He was breathless and his heavy coat was wet through by the time he had climbed the hill to the Keen council estate.

He slipped into the back porch and sat there for a while, feeling safe and secure for a moment. He looked at the geranium plants on the window sill, the one with the red bloom and the one with the blackcurrent coloured bloom. He hated the smell of them. They had the smell of death about them. He opened one of the top windows, but rain came in, so he closed it again, settled down in his deck chair and put up with the smell.

She heard him come in and brought him a cup of hot water and a can of lager. She didn't know which he would choose at this time of the day, so she brought both. He was bent over, reading his book, his *Great*

Expectations, which he had out from the library and kept renewing. She sat down with him for a while, but he was absorbed in his reading, his finger following the lines, and his coloured lenses over the print, which helped him overcome his dyslexia; so she sighed and went back to the kitchen. She remembered the black hair that had gone grey; the brown brooding eyes that had receded into watery meekness, the man who once turned all he touched into gold.

When she called him to dinner and he sat on the plastic chair at the tiny kitchen table, Irene had a good go at him. She was fretting because as soon as she had seen the first daffodil bloom, she had trudged up in the rain and mud to Halt Farm as she had done for the last thirty years. She was pleased because they would soon be paying as much as the new minimum wage, and the extra money was handy. There was new owners from up-country, and they was bound to be doing things right. Now, she was upset and disappointed because there was a big padlock on the gate and a scruffy cardboard notice nailed to a post: "NONE LOCAL DAFODILS PIKER WANTED."

Another woman in a headscarf and greatcoat was standing by the gate, looking up at the notice as well. They wondered what it meant. Without the local piece-workers, daffodils would soon be rotting in the fields.

"Does that mean 'none' or 'nine'?"

"None, by the size of the padlock."

"Not like when the Daniels was 'ere."

"Paid good money, they did."

"I use to earn thirty poun' a day."

111

"I use to earn thirty-five."

"Sometimes forty."

"Sometimes forty-five."

"Dependin'."

"Weather."

"Who're these new people got the daffodil farm, then?"

"Dunnaw. Foreigners from London."

"Ol' Daniel said twadn' profitable. Thas why 'e sold un to Londoners."

"With the minimum wage comin' in, an' all."

"Well, they got some bugger to do the pickin', any'ow."

"P'raps is a machine."

"P'raps 'tis, yow."

Irene laughed it off. "They 'ebm got no good grammar, any'ow."

"No, ner spellin'."

Irene told all of this to Dingo, in her declamatory style, reporting the conversation word for word, with all of the accompanying gestures.

Dingo made no reply. He grunted and left the table. He went back to the porch. Rain had begun to fall heavily again. It misted up the windows and merged the sea and the sky together. Even the coastline in the distance was obscured. He wondered when and where all of this would end, this life of his.

After doing the dishes, Irene came out to the porch and gave him hell. Why didn't he get a bleddy job and help her with the rates? She went on for ten minutes whilst he read his book. He loved the bit about Magwich, especially the part where he came back from Australia dressed as a farmer, where Pip didn't know that Magwich was his benefactor, and not the madwoman, but was soon to find out, through a series of careful questions posed by Magwich. What a thing that was. He sat pondering that great moment in the book, where the truth was revealed and all illusions were shattered. That was hard on Pip. Dingo wouldn't go about it that way.

After a while, he went into the kitchen and asked Irene if he could bring a motorbike into the front room. It was a big thing to ask, but well, it was a big job and it couldn't really be done out in the open, not with the rain coming down like it was at the moment. The rain hadn't stopped for weeks, on and off. He would put a lot of sacking down, so that the carpet wouldn't get ruined, and he would make sure the handlebars didn't ruin the wallpaper. He would put it on the stand.

Irene meant to say no, but she said yes. Her husband had a bike once, and 'ee done the same thing, didn''a?

She put her rubber boots in the back of the cupboard and Dingo gave her five pounds out of his unemployment benefit money to help to pay the rates, but it left him short of money and teasy and it left her still short as well. Her daffodil money normally paid the rates, and now she would have to go easy. He told her to stay away from the farm. They said in the pub, they got guns and fences and lights fit to land a plane up there.

"What? To keep the daffs in?"

Sometime later, Irene's boys came in from the pub. Dingo was asleep in the porch, his *Great Expectations* on the floor. Irene shut the door and served them in the kitchen.

"If the Krugerrands is still under the tarmac, there's no way to get they out. Not now."

"If the silly bugger tol' somebody before the tarmac was laid down."

"But 'ee didn' knaw us then."

"We was boys down school, then, when 'ee went to prison."

"Didn' even knaw there was a road."

"Not when 'ee was in the prison."

"You don't knaw nothin' when you git in there."

"Somebody should a visited un."

"Somebody from 'ere."

"'Ee employed a lot of people roun' 'ere."

"So 'ee did."

"Nothin'll shift they Krugerrands now."

'Ee'll never see they again."

"She could a done with they now."

Irene's boys felt sorry for their mother.

* * *

Jake went upstairs to see his mummy. He saw the glass and bottle beside the bed. The heavy curtains were drawn.

"You're in bed, Mummy."

"I know."

"Aren't you coming down for some tea? There's a new sponge cake with lemon butter icing. There's just me downstairs. Mrs Sawle is on her cigarette break."

"Revolting. No, I won't get up today. Why don't you bring yours up here?"

Jake thought about having to prepare a tray and then to take it a quarter of a mile up the broad, winding staircase with the blue carpet, through the heavy oak landing doors, down the long, polished hallway with the rucked and holed Persian rugs and runners. He decided against it.

"Why not come down, Mummy?"

"The Erard's action is all over the music room floor. Mr Blom says he has had to send to Leeds to have the bass strings made. He said he's never seen such a mess in an action. No wonder it's never played properly. No wonder the action has always been stiff and uneven. What did you do during the war, Grandpa Gruzelier? Oh, I didn't fight, no, I had the Erard's action done with the wrong springs that I got from the American officers who were billeted out on the downs. That's what I did for the war effort."

"You're angry with Grandpa Gruzelier, Mummy, for messing up your piano."

"No, I'm frustrated. I want to get on with my composition."

"You still have the Steinway, Mummy. There's still the Steinway in the long gallery. Mr Blom says it's tuned to Continental pitch and the Erard will only go to English pitch and that's why the choristers can't sing your treble lines."

"Mr Blom is a gorilla, not a musician. The Steinway was Aunt Agatha's. The Erard's sort of special, John. It was my own Mummy's. It came from Carlyon, and I brought it back to Carlyon."

"You never play it, though. You always play the Yamaha."

"Are you surprised?"

"How does your composition go, Mummy?"

"I don't know: I've forgotten. I've lost the thread now. And works of art don't go. They are works of art. My compositions are works of art, John. You should know that by now. They don't go."

Mummy was getting quarrelsome, so Jake thought he would go down and look at the horses. He started to sidle off.

"Think I'll go and look at Crackers, Mummy."

"His name is Hollywood Cotton Crackerjack, not Crackers. Don't get in front of him and don't get behind him: and Jake?"

"Yes, Mummy?"

"Whilst you're down there, see if Mr Curgenven will send up some of his "cure" to Mummy. Tell Mr Curgenven Mummy has a headache."

***

Hetty slid off the tallboy and was lucky to be heard by Ronnie Polglaze, who was looking for his coal money and just happened to open her bedroom door. In the hospital, Hetty Pengelly was surprised to find herself beside a young man. She thought she was dreaming, but the cleaner said no, they had all mixed wards these days. When Hetty thought on it, she said to herself, well, this was what comes of mixed schooling. This was the final outcome of all that. Hetty didn't agree with it in principle, but then, there was nothing wrong with a young man. He was quite compos mentis, unlike the others, and it wasn't for her to ask what was wrong with'n. He said he overdosed and she said yes, you got to be careful these days, with they modern drugs, and that was it.

One thing he said made Hetty think upon it. He said that he was in the army once, and they had night vision goggles now, so you didn't have to stop your look-out when it come to darkness.

Hetty couldn't believe it, hardly. But then, there was lots of signs and wonders all over. She remembered that they used these things for nature watching on the television. So really, hospital opened up a world of possibilities, and she was glad she landed up there. The young man said he might try and get her some, though it wouldn't be so easy, now he was a pensioned off war hero. Hetty didn't like to ask what war that was. Could be Bosnia, he said. He was from up-country: you could tell: you didn't have to ask'n. She wondered whether he had any place to go to, after hospital. Later on, he said he was called Stephen. Then he said he was called Michael, so you couldn't understand much about him, really. To keep her mind active, she pointed out Old Pard in the corner of the ward, back for the second time, with his sister visiting and the curtains half pulled across. She said they was some rich people really, but you'd never know it, not to look at them. They had a lot of nice things in their houses, down Hellick. Well, poor Old Pard's place had already been burgled the other day. Thieves took everything away that was worth taking. His sister couldn' tell 'im yet. Would break 'is 'eart in 'is condition. There was some 'ansome things in 'is sister's 'ouse called Rescorla, too.

* * *

Chapter Nine

*A seed hidden in the heart of an apple
Is an orchard invisible.*

Welsh proverb

Monday March the Twentieth

Dingo rode the motorbike up to the great iron gates of Carlyon. He dismounted and walked the last few yards. Bodruggan was in the driveway, leaning on a rake, admiring a pretty plant which had established itself in a ditch, about five foot tall, with a thick fleshy stem and broad leaves with blooms, pinkish red, rather like that those of a snapdragon. March was unusually warm, and the spring was forging ahead.

"'Ansome, idn'a?" Bodruggan said, pointing to the plant in the ditch.

"What is a? I never seen nothin' like that. What is a?"

"Dunno. Just appeared in the drain. Pretty, idn'a?"

The two men looked at each other through the bars of the gate a long time. "I brought little John's motor bike," Dingo said. "He come down to the caravan with the gearbox broke. I got a cog and got it all done. Is workin' all right." There was a silence between them. "So, could I speak to the little feller?"

Bodruggan seemed to be hesitating. "'Ee's not 'ere," he said. "'Ee's probably gone school again now."

"He was expelled from his school," Dingo said, with dignity. "He hasn't got a school to go to, not at the moment. He will soon, but jes for the moment 'ee's at home..."

"I'll take the bike," Bodruggan said, opening up one gate. "You send a' invoice. They'll pay. They'm good payers, you can count on that. Gwariors was alwees good payers."

"It didn't cost me much," Dingo said, "not the cog. Jes my time, and I got plenty of that." His eyes and his forehead pleaded with Bodruggan. "I'd just like to see un. Give the bike to'n myself, like. I done all the work for'n myself, see."

Old man Bodruggan looked all around him. He looked into Dingo's eyes, where he saw his own pain of being misunderstood and discounted. At last, thinking, well, the man wants to do the boy a favour. There aren't many of they about: "You come with me, Mr Dingle," he said.

Bodruggan scrunched across the gravel and went quickly into the bushes, Dingo following him with the Triumph. By a strange circuit, down paths and up mounds and overgrown shrubberies, they reached the old folly in the trees. Dingo remembered it. It had a trap-hatch that went down into an adit that led out to the sea caves, like the one he had in his own scrapyard, an age ago.

Bodruggan took the bike from him, unlocked the folly door and pushed it in to the musty room. "This is my folly now," Bodruggan said. "I bin coming 'ere for years, on an' off. There used to be a lot of activity 'ere, years ago. 'Course, a lot a fishin' is finished now, if 'ee d'knaw what I mean."

Dingo knew what he meant. "It was a long time ago," Dingo said.

"See," Bodruggan said, "the boy do come 'ere in th'afternoon, sometimes. I do brew up my tay and talk to'un. I like 'is company. 'Ee's a bright boy. 'Ee's lonely fer a boy. She never 'ad no more chillen, an..." He started to pour purple metholated spirit into the bowl of a Primus stove, and lit it. Dingo watched as the purple and gold flames warmed the vents at the top of the stove. The old man gave it a pump or two. The flames from the bowl died as the vapour lit, a perfect miniature gas stove. He put his blackened silver coloured singing-kettle on the jet. "Well, there you are then. Tea in a minute."

For the first time in many years, Dingo did not say, "I don't drink tea." Instead, he echoed, "Well, there you are then," and sat still and sighed, and thought about the son who was lost at sea.

They sat at the open door together, the magnificent fireplace by Henry Cleere and the winding stair that led to the toy battlements behind them. "I'm eighty, this year. 'Course, when I'm gone, I believe it will all crumble away, this buildin'. Because nobody do take any interest in ut but me. I don't think Mr. Gwarior knows is still 'ere. I try to tell the boy about it, about 'is great grandfather... He hesitated and looked straight at Dingo. 'Is great grandfather Gwarior, Dingo."

Dingo looked at his own hands.

There was another long silence between them as the Primus stove continued its little roar and the kettle began its first stirrings of song.

"See they rooks in the trees? They bin 'ere longer'n the Bodruggans. Sometimes the babies fall out a they trees an' I bind up a leg or a wing meself: I don't send them to no animal 'ospital. Sometimes they thrive, sometimes not. You can't never tell. I d' tell 'n 'bout the Bodruggans an' the civil war in Cornwall. I tell 'im 'ow my noble ancestor jumped the cliff. I tell 'im about the Grenvilles: people who are no mor'n 'is father's workmen now; but they're like the kind man at the foot of the rookery, bindin' up a leg or a wing. I tell 'im 'ow great estates are lost and won so easy, on the turn of a card. I tell 'im about the Carlyons and the Gwariors. I tell 'im 'ow 'is mother is the last of the Carlyons, and 'ow she married 'is father, and 'ow, through 'er, the Carlyons are back in Carlyon, just as the Lady Agather an' the verses foresaw. I tell over the verses to'n, but I don't tell'n all of the verses yet. Not the last verses: 'ee got to learn them gradual. "Blue and brown on the down..." I talk to'n about the gardens. 'Ow I planted they trees over there. 'Ow my father planted that walk over there. 'Ow my gran'father planted that avenue of oaks over there. Because we bin 'ere longer than the Gwariors. We bin 'ere nearly as long as the Carlyons. An' the Carlyons brung us 'ere, an' they hid us 'ere, as the civil war passed over our 'eads. So, as long as 'ee's a Carlyon, Dingo, 'ee's safe with me. People come an' go in this parish, Amos. Yer father, 'ee come over from Ireland, didn'a?

Lived out on the downs. People come an'go, Amos. People come an'go in this parish. But the Carlyons go on, see. 'Twas meant to be, 'is mother come back to Carlyon... How did 'ee move the stone, Dingo?"

His imagination still wandering around the corridors of history, if Dingo could have been caught out at that moment, he would have been. But Dingo replied softly, automatically, "The Coen stone? I never moved the stone. It moved itself. They do move themselves: stones like that. I could have done, with a digger an' a small crane. But I would've made a mess of the hedges and the land. There was no trace. The stone moved isself to the meadow, Arthur. Like they do. Iss the Coen Stone, the stone of the saint of the parish. Coen Stone tried to walk 'ome, back to the centre of the Round."

Bodruggan made no more of the stone. He pressed no further. The kettle boiled. Tea was made. Amos drank tea slowly. He took as long as he could over the tea, sipping and sipping air, as the afternoon ground on; until finally John Gwarior, his own son John appeared through the bushes and stood in front of them, his head cocked to one side, his black hair as black as the rook's, his riding coat and his riding boots too big for him.

Overcome with emotion, Dingo could hardly speak. The boy was more beautiful than he remembered, with his dark curls and his deep brown eyes. "I brought your bike", he said at last. "It's here in the folly. Mr Bodruggan put it here in the folly, behind us. I got it goin'. I bin all over Cornwall lookin' for a part. I stripped the gearbox down an'..." Dingo stood up and held out his arms.

"Oh shit, I forgot about that. I really don't want it, actually. I'm completely off motorbikes. Sorry, Mr Dingle. Bodruggan will settle up with you. Sorry."

For a moment, prep school manners dictated that the boy look sorry that he had inconvenienced Mr Dingle. Then he was off again through the rhododendron bushes, a small blush on his cheeks. Dingo found himself standing with his arms outstretched.

Bodruggan gathered up the mugs. He swilled them out with fresh water from the kettle and put the sugar bag back in its tin. He pricked the jets at the top of the Primus stove and put it away. Bodruggan looked up into the trees. "Is time to go now, Amos," he said.

"P'raps it is," Dingo said.

"As long as I 'ave breath in my body, I'll look after'n," Bodruggan said.

"An' after you've gone?"

There was no audible reply. "See that vine?" He said later. I nursed that vine. A branch can't bear fruit by isself: only if it remains in the vine."

Dingo went on in his own mind: 'I am the vine, and you are the branches. Whoever remains in me, and I in him, will bear much fruit; for you can do nothing without me.' But the Bodruggans were not Christ, and Dingo felt rebellion swell up. For a moment, he thought of just simply taking the boy away, to a place where they could just live together, where pagan magic didn't work; where Dingo would go to work for his boy, take him to the

Sunday school and begin all over again. Just like his own father did.

"Don't even think about it," Bodruggan's vine leaves seemed to whisper behind him.

Bodruggan locked up the folly and led Dingo back across the front lawn of the house in the full light of day. Dingo was surprised at that. He somehow assumed that he ought not to be here, though he had legitimate business with the motor bike. He could not help but look up at the windows of the principal rooms on the first floor. In Agatha's time he had been in the tower and in the ground-floor rooms that they always opened up for the estate Christmas party. He'd never seen the other rooms and wondered where, in this great mansion, the small Gwarior family would be living. Was it in Agatha's small flat on the first floor? Where was that located? Did it still exist? Most of the rooms seemed closed up and shuttered, unused, as they had been in Agatha's time.

Then he saw her. She was there. For a moment, he froze and stood rooted. In that moment, he took it all in: he saw Christice looking down at him, several feet from the window, heavier than before, now a big, busty, red-faced woman; but she could clearly be seen in her bedroom, in a brandy coloured, half-open housecoat, clutching a bottle and a glass. She looked aghast, as though she was witnessing a shaft giving way and falling in, taking the lawn with it. Dingo put down his head and plunged across the grass after Bodruggan.

Bodruggan saw her too, but he ignored the apparition. In an undertone, Bodruggan started to talk

125

about the cuckoo, a very pretty bird, a bird that sings as it flies; a bird that had just a very short space of time to lay its egg in a nest that didn't rightly belong to it; you couldn't talk about the cuckoo being in the wrong, because that was how the cuckoo was made; how the young cuckoo in the nest was blind, but had a ridge down its back for heaving out all the others and making a place for itself to stay and thrive in. You couldn't pass judgement on it: that was the way it was. The host parents went on feeding it, not knowin' nothin' 'bout ut. "It was the way God made the cuckoo, Dingo; an' every bird 'as 'is place in the sight a God."

As they stood at the great iron gates in the twilight, for some reason they almost shook hands, and were about to do something of the kind when a Land Rover came bearing down upon them from the direction of the old coach house, its headlights full on.

"Here comes Tregeagle," Bodruggan said, automatically sliding into the shallow ditch beside the drive, his hand going up towards his cap. Dingo followed him. They stood like a pair of schoolboys beside a clump of white and purple foxgoves, unseasonably in full flower already, as the imperious vehicle slowed down and stopped beside them.

The driver's window slid back. A nose poked out and addressed itself to Dingo. "Who are you?"

"Amos Dingle, come to deliver John Gwarior's repaired motor bike."

"See him off, Bodruggan."

"Right you are," they replied automatically, in unison.

Then Bodruggan rose up and said, with great dignity, "Wait there, Mr Dingle."

In the headlights, Arthur Bodruggan undid the gates slowly and methodically whilst Dingo looked on from his position in the gutter, in misery. When both gates were fully open, and Bodruggan was satisfied, Bodruggan gestured to him. He escorted Dingo through the gates, in the centre of the drive.

"Don't forget," he said under his breath, "I'll look after'n like my own. 'Ee's a Carlyon, don't forget. She bred them out and brought 'im back to Carlyon an' they don't know it. Thas all. Now don't bugger it up, or you really will be seen off. There's a lot ridin' on ut. Walk tall, Dingo, you done a good night's work, that time. When you do hear the cuckoo, open a bottle, raise yer glass an' 'ave a good laugh. The Gwariors are jiggered, an' they don't know it. You're a lucky man, Amos. One day, that boy will get the keys to the cellars and the folly: an' thas the key to Carlyon: you don't need me t' tell you that. So take heart, because up there, where white is black and black is white, you won."

"But will you tell'n? Will you ever tell'n about me? 'Ee's got a right to know. 'Ow will 'ee ever know?"

"'Ee'll knaw, all in good time. 'Ee went need me to tell'n. I'll soon be gone, but 'ee'll live on in Carlyon; an' so will 'is own sons, an' 'is sons after they. Only 'is name is wrong. Is a small sacrifice to keep 'im in Carlyon 'till the Gwariors are dead an' gone. 'Ee'll change 'is name to

Carlyon, when the time d' come. Don't bugger it up, Dingo. Let it work. Now listen to me, Amos, this is the 'ard part. Is time t'get away an' let it work. Keep in the middle of the road, my 'ansome, an' keep gwoin'. An' don't look back. 'Ave a drink to the cuckoo tonight, Amos, an' don't look back. You know what you got t'do. Because if you don't, everything will be swept away in the storm that will follow after 'ee."

Bodruggan pushed Dingo outside the iron gates, locked them up and got into the Land Rover beside Henry's land agent. They turned a circle and swept up the drive, leaving Dingo in darkness. The large, pretty plant which Bodruggan and Dingo so admired earlier in the day, bowed and curtsied to the movement of air that the big vehicle had disturbed, suddenly exploding a seed or two into the soil, all at the wrong time of the year. It seemed to be smirking, but no-one saw; and in any case that was an illusion of the night, because, as everyone knows, whilst plants may almost glow with well-being at having established themselves in a good environment, they have no sense of humour and are incapable of knowing what success they may be about to achieve in driving out the natives in a foreign land.

"What were you saying to that man Dingle?" The agent asked Bodruggan. "I've never seen Mr Gwarior so angry. He was incandescent with rage after Mrs Gwarior telephoned him in the estate office."

"Aw, I told Dingo one 'r two things, fer 'is own good. 'Ee went bother Mr an' Mrs Gwarior again. They c'n be sure a that. They c'n rely on ol' Bodruggan. You tell 'em, Bodruggan will put things right. Bodruggan d'knaw where all the drains is. Make sure you tell 'em, pertic'ler. Bodruggan d'knaw where all the drains is."

Drains? What was Bodruggan on about now? This was the most peculiar estate he'd ever seen, where the pensioned-off gardener seemed to dictate policy and everything else from a derelict folly in the bushes, because he knew where the drains were. The agent had never known anything like it. How the family had survived this long, he couldn't imagine. Cornwall was a very odd place. Very, very odd.

Dingo kept walking in the centre of the road until the headlights behind him were gone. Then he stopped to wait for his night vision to come, turned around and followed the great brick wall of Carlyon for nearly a mile, over fields, over hedges and through ditches, stopping only to get his breath and re-orient himself. After a while, the wall gave way to an overgrown Ha-Ha, and then to plain high hedges, with worn, low places made by the badgers, where people came and went. He sat in one of these, under a thorn bush for an hour or two, quite still, until he was satisfied that there was no dog, no goose, no nothing to wake to his soft tread. There was a strong smell of fox in this corner of the park; and where the fox went, he knew he was safe in hiding. Then he moved up slowly towards the house, keeping in the shadows, all the while.

He watched the weary housekeeper and her husband trek through the house, putting the lights on and off. He sensed the heavy wooden shutters straining on their old hinges; twenty, thirty times, he heard the metal bar swing across and down into the iron bracket, shutting out people like him. One by one, the lights went out in all the far corners of the building, leaving the world to the fox and to Dingo. Here, in front of the house where his son slept, he could think it all out. The rhododendrons covered him.

The old moon came up, but it was a strange, strange moon. It hovered about as though it knew that something was going to happen to it. And as Dingo watched through the hours, sure enough, the moon turned red for a while, a dog moon with the shade of the moving earth upon it. It measured the time for him. No-one came out on the terrace to look at it through their telescope. He thought of how long life was, and how short it was. He thought of how we are all here and gone so quick, and how most of us leave no trace of our passing. Unseen, the earth moved on; the moon cleared of its red shadow and all of nature sighed and perked up and carried on with its night work. Still Dingo sat on in the hedge, not feeling the cold.

In the middle of the night, when the moon was bright, a light snapped on in Henry's office downstairs. Dingo felt compelled towards it, through loneliness and curiosity, through the lack of something to do. There were no shutters in the room. Modern security bars had replaced them, though that was a silly thing, Dingo thought. If you wanted to get in, you would get in through the kitchen, where there was a window left open in the laundry. You would slip down the corridors and crowbar your way into the office, easy enough.

With a terrible rush of the senses, he saw the child start up Henry's computer and sit, completely absorbed.

Life as a scrap metal merchant, and life as a prisoner had taught him all about the manipulations of others for their own ends. He knew Bodruggan's game. Bodruggan was only kept alive by the thought that the Gwariors were already bred out of Carlyon without their knowing it. Well, that may be so. It may be as simple as that. But it may not be, yet. The Gwariors were capable of doing away with Dingo's son when they found out: of shooting him down like a pheasant, after they'd bred him up. He didn't trust it.

Christice couldn't be relied on to keep her mouth shut, not forever, not when the going got rough. His one glimpse of that great, blowsy figure in the window told him that, the instant he clapped eyes on her. She would start squawking, the minute the booze dried up, he could see that: he'd seen that sort of thing before. And with the alcohol sloshing around, with a filthy temper, and with a peck of spite, she was stupid enough to betray herself, any time. He saw what happened this afternoon. He'd put two and two together already. She panicked when she saw him on the lawn, and she got him removed from the grounds quick, before she could be blamed. He could see it all. She'd kept her head long enough to work her ticket with Henry. That got her and the boy into Carlyon. Now she had to stay there for the next twenty, thirty years: and that was something else. Day in, day out, living with a lie;

living with a whopper. Not everybody could do that: very few. What got men into prison? Talking got men into prison. Boasting, bragging, it was incredible how many hardened criminals suffered, day in, day out, from their conscience, and from blabbing at the wrong time, often just as they were home and dry. There were very few born without a conscience. He had come across a few, heard their versions of things. The psychopath was always recognisable. Christice Gruzelier, with her bottle and her glass, was not one. He didn't know much about people like Henry Gwarior. He never mixed with their class. But what he did know was that Henry would put up with Christice and the boy as long as he believed the boy was a Gwarior. Once he knew the truth, Henry would act.

Was it true what Bodruggan said? That the young cuckoo in the nest had a ridge down its back for heaving out all the rest? Was that just a bit of nonsense? How much sense of self-preservation would the boy have? Dingle genes would give him what? Make him able to live out on the downs? Make him able to drink and swear and collect scrap metal? Make him a murderer, capable of revenge? He'd already burnt his school down. What more would he do?

What would Agatha have said about this bitter mess? "Well, this is what comes of incontinence, Amos Dingle." Lady Agatha would never have believed in verses and predictions and mumbo jumbo. Agatha was a Christian woman, out to preserve Carlyon. She'd married a Gwarior: she didn't give a damn who was left in charge after her, as long as the building and a family survived in it. She put her duty first, and her vision was as narrow as anybody's.

What would Jesus have said? "Go and sin no more, son."

But what did you do about the seed that you had already sown?

Henry had accepted the boy as his own son. So be it. So far, so good. Dingo could come up here, any time, in the dark, to take a peep at his son. He would be able to read the newspaper and see the photos in the paper when John found a bride. He could leave the caravan by the roadside, do what the probation officer said and live quietly with Irene, keep a low profile, see how the land was lying, make himself known to the boy when and how he wanted to. He could walk miles to watch the boy riding his horse at the meet. And perhaps his Krugerrands would turn up again. The main thing was, he could be on hand to intervene if things started to go very bad for John.

That was it, then: there was no reason why he should not stay here quietly, living out his life in the parish, secretly watching over his son. But then he thought of Bodruggan's narrow vision and saw in an instant why he had been led across the lawn to confront Christice at her window. It was Bodruggan's tom-foolery; Bodruggan's arrogance and pride and self-confidence; his thoughtless self-interest. It was in Bodruggan's interests to get Dingo seen off the land and run out of the parish. He was a dangerous old man; a word here, a word there and Dingo's licence for freedom hung by a thread, with the Probation Service always at his back. John was

Bodruggan's cuckoo, not Dingo's. Bodruggan took matters in his own hands to keep Dingo out. John was Bodruggan's dream of a Carlyon, back in Carlyon. That was what they were all doing there, working for a pittance, Mee and Grenville and Basset, all feeding and growing on the Gwariors, putting their suckers down and strangling them, all watching the ancient predictions work themselves out, because they were still loyal to the Carlyons and wanted them back in Carlyon. They were still in the Civil War and they were still in pagan times, worshiping rocks and stones. Bodruggan didn't give a damn about Dingo and his boy. Bodruggan would rather Dingo was gone, off the planet, back in prison for theft or something small, out of the equation. Well, that was all right: Dingo had to be wary of Bodruggan, that was all. Now that Dingo knew Bodruggan's vision, saw with Bodruggan's eyes, even Bodruggan could be manipulated.

But all the time, there was that innocent boy, knowing nothing of this, the blind fledgling in the nest. What was best for the boy? Did the boy have a ridge down his back for heaving out the others? You never saw the old cuckoo stay around the nest it stole. It never sat on an egg. It never knew whether its young survived or not: it was gone on its way.

But Dingo was not a cuckoo, driven by automatic responses; Dingo was a man, and men were born with conscience and duty and forethought and all the other things that made up a Christian life.

"So then," Dingo whispered to the night, "I got two ways: to stay or to go. Here he is, in front of me. I can take a few paces forward, knock on the window, frighten the life out of him, calm him down, talk to him, tell him who I am, before anybody else does. And then, he is burdened with it: burdened forever with the same strain of living the lie that is destroying his mother. So, what will knowledge of the secret do to him? How will he like to be the son of the murderer who lives in the caravan by the by-pass? Will he invite me up to his nursery for tea every Sunday? Show me his trains? Will he, hell? There's only one way, and that is to go, while he still thinks he's Henry Gwarior's son."

For an instant, the child looked up from his computer screen. He looked out into the creepy darkness of the terrace with its cracked stone flowerpots and its steps down to the lawn, and he seemed to smile an innocent, dreaming smile.

Dingo hesitated, folded his son's smile into his heart, and crept away.

Yet, out of sight of the house, slipping over the hedge again, he half turned and snarled savagely to the night, "But it's still a lie. It's still a dirty, stinking lie. And it will never do."

* * *

Chapter Ten

Keep a green tree in your heart,
And perhaps a singing bird will come.

Chinese proverb

Friday March the twenty-fourth

Hetty was struggling with Stephen Michael's army binoculars when the young man came in with his friend. Hetty wasn't all that pleased he come with his friend. She liked to give him tea and Terry's chockie bickies on his own. Anyway, it was lovely to have, as a present, another pair of binoculars with night vision.

The night vision binoculars kept Hetty busy whilst Stephen Michael's friend rifled through her bedroom drawers and took away her Timex watch and old paste engagement ring, not worth having. But there it was, she was sorry to lose her jewellery, and locked all the doors from then on.

* * *

Christice called in Nanny Sarah and sacked her on the spot.

She enjoyed doing that. She would like to have fired Arthur Bodruggan as well, for trailing Dingo across the front lawn in front of her bedroom windows and through the house. What on earth did Bodruggan think he was doing, the other day? She rang Henry on his mobile instantly and told him that she had just seen the murderer, Dingo in the bushes, probably thieving tools from the sheds. And was Henry aware that the *Atco Royale* lawnmower had already disappeared, this week? Well, she had to make sure that Henry knew that Dingo coming onto the estate was nothing to do with her. Seeing Dingo standing on the lawn outside had made her feel quite ill. Anyway, she already knew she couldn't fire Bodruggan for associating with Dingo, much as she would like to, because for some reason Henry wouldn't hear of it. Apparently, Bodruggan was the only one who knew where the drains were, Henry said, this morning. You couldn't upset Bodruggan, so you had to pay the ghastly little man a pension for the rest of his life. Aunt Agatha had arranged it all, out of some secret fund. And you had to be quiet and not tell him off. She did get him into the music room today, though, where she posed casually on her round piano stool with her manuscript paper and her pencil, composing a new piece for piano and falsetto, and told him he was never to let Dingo nor any other tramp into the grounds again. She was quite taken aback when she got a mouthful of cheek from Bodruggan, something about it being very difficult indeed to separate Dingo from these grounds now, and she might have thought about that before she brought the boy to Carlyon; but she ignored him and sent him out quickly, hoping he didn't mean what she thought he might have meant. Not that Bodruggan could possibly know anything that happened between herself and Dingo, one drunken night, years and years ago, when Henry was regularly misbehaving himself. Still, Bodruggan's words gave her a jolt.

Certainly, it was Nanny Sarah's fault for not keeping an eye on the boy, and for letting him get into the clutches of Bodruggan and the other groundsmen, who filled his mind with absolute rubbish. You had to keep little John away from people like that, now that he was growing up. It was all right whilst he was still a baby. Bodruggan was always pulling John out of the ponds and bringing him back to the house to be cleaned up and dried out, when he was a baby. But not now, not when he was at an impressionable age. He'd already got into so much trouble at that draconian school, which was why he was still here at home in the middle of the term. She blamed the influence of these ignorant gardeners, and told Henry so. But Henry didn't want to listen to her, oh no.

Anyway, having fired Nanny Sarah, Christice was now going to be able to do the thing that she did so very well, which was to telephone *The Lady*, place an ad, await replies, schedule a ship-load of interviews and then interview a number of girls for the post. And she was very very good at interviewing. Because what she did, and this was the clever part: she always offered the prospective, unsuspecting nannies a glass of wine, and then if any girl said yes, well then, that girl was completely out of the running. A few of them fell for it every time. Because nannies mustn't drink, on or off duty; not in front of little John.

She pulled up and down on the drawstrings of the curtains until she managed to get them closed. She lay down on the bed for a while because the sunlight hurt her eyes in the afternoon. What the hell was Dingo doing up here with Bodruggan? John must be kept in the house. Now she'd fired Nanny Sarah, she'd better get on with interviewing some more nannies. She'd better telephone *The Lady* now. She didn't see how she could keep John confined to the house, otherwise. Of course, he really needed a tutor: that would keep him busy and organised. What business could Dingo possibly have up here? Oh, how embarrassing. He couldn't come here. This house wasn't a tourist attraction. It wasn't open to the public. Not yet, thank God. Agatha had stinted herself all those years, and just when Henry was going white at the thought of inheriting a pile of debt, what happened? A mountain of cash was found. The strongroom contained a mountain of cash in Tesco shopping bags. Coming from God knows where. Just good housekeeping, she had to suppose. God knows. Did Agatha have her own money? Well, what ever the old girl had been doing, the secret died with her. There were a lot of secrets here: the Gwariors had a hell of a lot of secrets that she, a Carlyon, wasn't ever let into. Not even one of the portraits on the stairs was of a Carlyon, and the Carlyons built the wretched house. Typical. That mountain of cash must have been going down ever since, along with the tarnished Victorian silverware and the bijou portfolio of hopeless stocks and shares: even that revolting Gilles had been able to go off to Morocco on a comfortable lump sum. A pension here, a pension there, all had to be honoured by Henry. What did Gilles do to deserve a pension? And now, Henry had to pay for it. Well, it wasn't fair. Poor Henry.

Anyway, she was sure there was sufficient cash to pay for a tutor and a new nanny. She couldn't manage without a tutor and a new nanny. She would get on with it right away. But first, Christice had half a glass of vodka with some orange. Then she fell asleep on the bed, because things were all too difficult and the afternoon sun was altogether too strong for her eyes.

* * *

Hetty watched a young man rifle through some nudists' clothes and wondered whether he would take all their clothes away, but he didn't seem to. She wondered whether he got their car keys too.

The trouble with watching life from up here was that you could never know the outcome of anything. It was as bad as fetching a newspaper every day. You could only see little bits and pieces. Snatches of things. But you never saw the end of anything. You could only imagine what happened next. She supposed that on the beach, you could see everything. But then, you were too close to it all on the beach, and you could only see the sand that somebody's kid kicked in your face.

* * *

After John discovered that Nanny Sarah had packed her bags and had gone, he knew that he had only a few days of complete freedom before another nanny appeared. The first thing he did was go to his Mummy's purse in the afternoon when she was out for the count, as his father called it, and grab a ten pound note. Then, he got past the land agent, who was fiddling with something at his desk in the coach house, strolled down the long bridle path, across the stiles and into the village. There, he was able to stock up on tuck. He missed the tuck shop, now that he was away from school. Margaret Pengelly's Spar Shop in the village had a few cheap boiled sweets and a lolly fridge but there weren't many quality chocs there. He loaded up with some Mars Bars and Twixes, coming out into the sunlight just as Kevin and Darren were going in. He didn't notice them particularly, but they noticed him.

Instead of robbing Margaret's, they decided to rob John. He looked like an easy target, with his bulging bag of cream eggs and expensive choc'lets. When they saw that the boy was taking a lonely path over the stiles, Kevin raced across the fields with Darren following behind. As John came up to them, they were sitting in a hedge, Darren whittling away at a stick with his knife, achieving the nonchalant, menacing look; Kevin thinking of various openings for making his intentions known to the victim.

John was under orders not to talk to boys from the village, but he had been looking for an opportunity to make friends down there. These two seemed like young versions of Shaun Mee, so they must be all right. "Hello, hello," he said, climbed up and sat down in the hedge with them, immediately opening up his bag of goodies and spreading his chocs on the stones.   "I've just bought these," he said. "Turn out your bags, share out and share about."

Darren gawped, whilst Kevin said, "No no, you're all right. We didn' buy none." He refused the Twix he was offered, right off.   You never took sweets from strange boys, when you don't know them, not just like that.   He slapped Darren's hand as it reached out for a Yorkie Bar; but John indicated, no, the chocs are all unadulterated, so tuck in, chaps.

"I don't suppose you got a Rizla?" Kevin said.

"Yes, here you are."   John took out the tobacco and the orange packets of Rizlas that Shaun Mee was always leaving around on the benches in the sheds.

Darren took one or two books of papers automatically and stuffed them in his pocket.

"What you called?" Kevin enquired.

"My name is Jake."

"Where you live?"

"Over there."

"Over where?"

"There. Beyond the trees."

"What: in the lodge?"

"No, not quite."

"So where?"

"Well, in the big house, actually."

"Carlyon Big House?"

"Yes, actually."

Darren exploded: "What?   In that great 'ouse with all the windas?   I seen it one time, Kev."

Kevin said, suspiciously, "Wot, you live in the Big House?"

"No, not in all of it. We live in just a small part of it."

"Part of it?"

"It's too big for the family to live in all of it."

Kevin and Darren exchanged a glance.

"Ideal."

"What do you do with the bit you don't live in, then?"

"It's under dust sheets, for most of the year."

"Dust sheets?" Darren looked at Kevin for guidance on this one.

"Dust sheets fer the painters," Kevin said, nodding knowledgeably.

"Don't you 'ave no lodgers?"

"No, no lodgers. Well... housekeeper's husband, who doubles as a driver and caretaker, but isn't paid anything. I suppose he might be considered a sort of lodger. Cousins used to come down for the summer in Carlyon's heyday. We haven't any cousins now, not living in this country, anyway."

"Oh 'es. My cousins d'come down in the heyday. So, where you go school, Jake?"

"I used to go to school in Somerset, but I won't be going back there any more."

"Somerset," Darren said. "I bin there."

"'Ow's that, then? Why aren't you gwoin back school up Somerset?"

"I burnt it down."

144

There was silence.   They thought about it for a while, licking out a cream egg.

"Cool," they said together.

Jake got to his feet and looked at his watch, which Kevin noticed at once and thought, oo, what a really tasty sports watch with towellin' round the strap, but didn't say nothin'. "Better go. Make myself visible," Jake said.

"What?"

"'Ee idn' allowed out long. 'Ee'll be missed, at 'ome, you stoopid cuckoo." Darren really let Kevin down sometimes.

"Will 'ee be out tomorrow?"

"I'll be safe for a few days; until they get me a new nanny."

"A new what? A new nanny?" Darren rolled over onto his back, kicking his legs up in the air, convulsed with laughter. "A new fuckin'nanny?"

"Darren calls 'is mad ol' granny 'is nanny."

"Oh I see. Is Darren dyslexic?"

"No, Jake, 'ee's a bit thick."

The two bright boys laughed, whilst Darren recovered his composure. Then John went on up the lane, carrying every scrap of litter from the chocolate feast.

Wandering back to the village over the roadway fields, Kevin said, "Shit, Darren, dat is one dane druss motherfucker. 'Ee burnt 'is school down, up Somerset."

* * *

Christice woke up with a start. She heaved herself out of bed. Time to get up. It was after five. Henry would be in soon, and Martin would be arriving at seven. That gave her two hours to shower, dress and see to her hair and face; but first, she must just go down and make sure that Mrs Sawle had left everything in order. Putting on a fairly simple shift dress, she found some shoes, grabbed her greasy glass and wobbled down the main stairs, a little unsteadily.

Christice still loved Fridays. It was a nice pretend end of the week, though everybody knew that on a busy estate there was never a weekend as such. There was always something going on at weekends, what with all the eventing and the shooting parties. In fact, weekends were more busy than weekdays, usually. Thank goodness there was enough money in the kitty to keep staff. But it was always such fun on a Friday evening. Henry insisted that little John wear a white shirt, jacket and tie; Henry and Martin dressed properly and Christice wore a good frock with a half decent piece of jewellery. It was the family getting together, and that was very, very important, as Henry always said.

There were some nice meaty smells coming from the kitchen. Mrs Sawle had been cooking the silverside on a low temperature for most of the afternoon; the vegetables were all chopped up and ready for the saucepans and the dining table had been laid for four. A cold pudding, cheese, bickies and coffee things had been left on the sideboard. All she had to do now was make the gravy for the beef. Even the packet of granules had been left out on the counter.

Coming through into the kitchen, she heard the sound of the housekeeper's little black and white television, which the housekeeper kept in the tiny parlour that used to be the butler's room in the old days. Mrs Sawle liked to keep a television handy, in case she missed something on the news, during her terribly long days on duty in the house, apparently. Anyway, the housekeeper's television was quite useful for little John, when he was being looked after by Mrs Sawle, during the times when there was no nanny.

Christice turned up the heat in the oven, so that the joint of beef would crisp nicely, and the roast potatoes would brown. She would do the vegetables soon. There was no rush yet. Vegetables should always be *al dente*.

Not being able to remember having a drink all day, Christice thought she would just have a glass of something before getting on with making the gravy. She put some orange juice in a tumbler, sipped a bit, thought, "Oh lor, very tame," and added some vodka, a generous splosh. She called to little John, who had just come in through the kitchen door with a bag of silver chocolate wrappers for "Save the Children." "Goodness," she exclaimed, "what have you got on your jeans? Grass? Better have a shower and get into your smart mufti now, because Daddy will be in soon and Martin will be here for dinner as usual." As he went out, muttering, she called him back. "Oh do look at this, John."

On the television, there was a frightfully interesting programme on elephants and conservation. It was a sort of news programme for children. Christice was sure that it would be of great interest to John, and made him sit down with her on the housekeeper's little chintz sofa to watch it.

After his mummy had topped up her glass a few times, John was able to slip out of the parlour, through the kitchen, down the long corridor and into Daddy's business room, where he could play games on the office computer. Mummy didn't notice for some time that John had disappeared; and when she did, she imagined he had probably gone up to his room to have a shower and change his clothes.

The children's news programme ended, and a favourite Australian soap opera came on. She just wanted to know what was happening; then she would go up and change. She topped up her drink.

After that came the real news. That was so gloomy, it deserved a top-up. She sat through that: nothing of real interest. She couldn't be bothered with the regional news, so she heaved out of the chair and climbed up the back stairs to her bedroom to change.

It was probably too late for a shower, so she had a bit of a wash and looked for a frock that hadn't been shrunk by the dry-cleaners or the laundry. Having found a dress that still fitted, she put on her face, untangled her hair with a comb a bit and went down.

After looking at some plans in the estate office, Henry came into the house and looked into the dining room. He liked Fridays: he liked having his cousin, Martin's company, once a week. The sideboard was in order; the table was correct; the room was spotlessly clean. He decided to open the bottle of red wine to let it breathe whilst he went up and changed his clothes.

Looking in the sideboard drawer for a corkscrew, he became aware of a burning smell. Sighing, "Oh no, not again," he stepped quickly across the hall and into the kitchen. Noticing that the vegetables were still lying in neat piles beside the saucepans, he turned off the heat before he opened the main oven door swiftly and stood back, as hot blue and black smoke billowed out at him.

Surveying the damage quickly, checking the time on his watch, he went to the telephone and dialled Mrs Sawle's number. He let the telephone ring for a long time, whilst he thought about what he should do next. It was half past six; Martin would be here at seven. Mrs Sawle was clearly "not at home." He didn't blame her: it was her time off. After going to the sink and scrubbing his hands, he started hunting around for some cold food in the refrigerator.

After a few minutes, the telephone rang. It was Mrs Sawle. "You rang?" She enquired, icily.

"Mrs Sawle, I'd be very grateful if you would come down and prepare some food for us. The beef appears to be burnt and inedible."

"I see," she said. "I was just on my way out to enjoy the very few hours of sunlight between now and lockup."

Mrs Sawle made a delicious soup out of the vegetables she had left by the saucepans, and stayed on to serve it and clear away. Then, at nine o'clock, Christice told her very graciously that she might go now, because they could manage with the cold meats, the remains of a pork pie and salads.

Christice managed a small glass of wine. Martin noticed that she gulped it down. Little John took all of the pork pie and turned up his nose at the dry meats and the salads. Henry made a remark or two about that. Christice ignored him and pointedly talked very brightly to Martin about her new composition, which she intended to dedicate to the dear little Cathedral Choristers, who would probably perform it at some point.

As soon as Mrs Sawle left the room, Christice launched a broadside on the housekeeper, saying that the woman was useless: she had burnt the silverside and that was why John didn't eat much.

Henry remarked that John had, in fact, scoffed all the pork pie, leaving none for anybody else. "What exactly did happen in the kitchen this afternoon? The explanation I received from Mrs Sawle was quite different."

"Oh?"

"Yes, Christice, please can you explain."

Martin studied the wallpaper, feeling uncomfortable. He remembered, there used to be brown cupids in relief on the original sepia coloured wallpaper, but there was now a muddy sort of pub wallpaper, approved by the Heritage people. There had been a protracted row about it, he seemed to remember, and a fragment of the original wallpaper had been preserved in a glass case somewhere. .

"Well, Mrs Sawle put the beef on at the wrong temperature for hours and it burnt whilst I was upstairs trying to get changed."

"This does not agree with Mrs Sawle's account of the matter. Mrs Sawle said that she put the beef in the oven at a low temperature at three o'clock, before going off duty. She stated that she prepared everything as usual; and that I could certainly see when I came in. Everything was as it should be. Indeed, I find that Mrs Sawle is very good on detail. She is a fine housekeeper. You are expected to come down early in the evening, before changing, and make the final preparations for the meal. I saw that the vegetables had been prepared; the gravy was waiting to be made; there was very little left to do. So what happened this time?"

Christice reached across the table for a bottle of wine.

"Yes, and that, Christice, is the root of the problem, isn't it."

"Excuse me," Christice said graciously, and walked out, carefully, avoiding the chairs.

There was a pause, after which Martin enquired whether there had been any success in getting rid of the Japanese Knot Weed.

"Well, of course," Henry replied quite quietly, "we obtained the ministry leaflet about it, as you will remember, but I'm afraid Bodruggan doesn't read anything but seed and cuttings catalogues and, well, not to put too fine a point on it, I understand that he sent Basset and Mee down to the edge of the woodland, where they hacked at it a bit and left the cut stems lying there beside the pond. They sprouted, rooted and now we have a real problem. It's like the many-headed Hydra down there."

"But that was only a few months ago."

"I know. It was a surprise to see what had happened. It's not often that I walk down there."

"This is now a job for the professionals, I suppose."

"Apparently so."

"No sign of the Himalayan Balsam plant in Cornwall?"

"Not yet, no. But it will come. As I understand it, it came in with the flax to the cotton mills and proceeded down the canals and waterways. The Balsam is destroying the bluebell woodlands in Yorkshire. It is believed to be profoundly altering the understorey flora and fauna in the deciduous woodland of Western Europe. It's a real plague."

Henry seemed thoroughly fed up and depressed by the alien species at Carlyon.

When Christice took her seat at the table again, new plantings in the park were being discussed. Henry was saying that he must give instructions to Bodruggan to have the Rhododendron cut back because it had now begun to encroach on the ride. It was beginning to grow right out of control.

"Do you think that Polycarpus would survive here?" Martin asked brightly. "It's growing successfully at Trelowarren, on the Lizard."

"But that's on the Lizard, isn't it," Henry said, irritably.

"Well, let's ask Bodruggan about this."

"I like the Rhododendron," Christice butted in, crisply. "I don't want it cut back. John likes to make his dens in it."

"We have to leave the management of the gardens to Bodruggan. I feel we do have to open up a vista from the house to the ride."

"Oh, we have to leave it to Bodruggan, do we? We have to ask Bodruggan whether we may open up a vista from the house to the ride, do we? And then what do we have to ask Bodruggan, after we've asked about the vista and the ride? Do we then have to ask him about the Polythinggy? Where may we plant that, Mr Bodruggan?"

"Christice, he is our gardener and groundsman."

"And he knows where all the drains are, does he?"

Martin looked up from his scrutiny of the dregs at the bottom of his empty wine glass. "If I might say something, Christice: Bodruggan is a key person on the estate. We cannot do without Arthur Bodruggan."

"He's a nasty, insolent octogenarian who ought to be pushing up the daisies from the other side of the lawn."

She liked her turn of phrase so much, she said it twice more. "He's too big for his boots and I want him off the estate."

"And this, we cannot do," Henry said quietly.

"Why the hell not? Are you running this estate, or is he?"

The men exchanged a glance, uncomfortably shifting in their chairs.

"Bodruggan stays, whether we like it or not."

"Why? Why does Bodruggan have to stay?"

"Drains."

"Cool," little John muttered under his breath. "Ideal."

The child was ignored, but Martin wondered for a moment where he picked up his strange vocabulary.

There was a silence, during which Christice emptied the last of the wine from the two bottles into her glass, creating a pink concoction.

"You're afraid of that little man, aren't you? Well, I'm not. I'm the bloody Carlyon here, and I'll see to him, if you're so weak."

"If you value your present way of life, you must not."

"I must not what? What?"

"You must never interfere with Bodruggan, Christice."

"I agree with Henry," Martin said. "You must leave Bodruggan alone. We may not understand why, but that's the way it is."

Christice finished the wine and looked around the table for another bottle. There was only a bottle of Jolly Fizzy water. She grabbed for that. "I'm never told anything," she muttered. "And you two are starting to look older than any of the portraits of your ghastly family on the stairs." That was telling them.

Christice thought about her encounter with Bodruggan today by the piano. She couldn't remember clearly what it was that he said to her. She knew it was some sort of malicious threat and she remembered that she would have to shut up, but she couldn't remember for the life of her what it was all about. She contented herself with muttering over again that nobody ever told her anything; nobody consulted her; nobody asked her opinion; she was just a drudge in the house of her own ancestors.

She was ignored.

The row flared up once more when John got up from his chair without a word, the meal not yet finished, and started pacing up and down the dining room, having a boyish conversation with himself, gesticulating and mumbling. Henry noticed that he was wearing jeans soiled with grass and that his dirty trainers had deposited a trail of mud all over the Isfahani carpet. Henry said that John was turning into an absolute tramp and needed discipline. It was a constant battle to try and guard even the most basic of standards here.

Christice said it was time to get a new nanny and John also needed a tutor to keep him busy, since he couldn't go back to school, because he was coming too much under the influence of guess who? Guess who? Bodruggan and his ilk.

At that moment, John emerged from his pretend conversation with Kevin and Darren. He really loved Bodruggan and his friends on the estate as much as he really hated his embarrassing mother; and he could certainly do without Daddy and Martin's interference. For no reason, just to stop the row, he said, "You can't fire Bodruggan, Mummy, not like you fire all my nannies, because Bodruggan could certainly put Daddy in prison, easy as that." He clicked his fingers and for once, they snapped like a neck.

The men sat stock still. There was a stunned silence, after which he adamantly refused to listen to the pleadings of his mother to be a good boy, or go back to the table to sit with her; so he walked out, and to his surprise and pleasure, nobody tried to prevent him. He had no idea why his words had such an effect: Daddy had gone pale and Martin looked as though he had been struck on the back of the head. He thought he should certainly keep that little remark in reserve for a similar time.

After a few more minutes' silence around the table, Christice said she had had enough as well, and went upstairs to her room, with a headache.

Sitting together in Henry's study, Henry made his apologies to Martin, saying that Christice was not as she used to be when they were young. Indeed, none of them were quite the same as when they were young, more's the pity. He went on to apologise about his seeming obduracy on the matter of Bodruggan and to thank Martin for supporting him this evening on what was quite a difficult matter "...You couldn't possibly know, Martin, but by the way Aunt Agatha left things, it has never been possible simply to retire Bodruggan, as such. The estate was almost bankrupt, and Agatha put things on a different footing. Although I would rather we did not, yet still we do owe a great debt to Bodruggan. I came into the estate ill prepared. I could not have known what was involved. It is not my fault and there is nothing I can do about the way things are. You know the saying attached to this house, 'When the mantle falls to the heir, the arms will appear.'... or is it mantlet? You think it's nothing, but then... you can never know until the keys are in your hands. Perhaps I am a weak man, I don't know..."

Martin nursed his brandy glass throughout Henry's faltering speech. Martin knew something about the adit under the folly, and wondered about it, but yet he was still innocent of any knowledge of the tunnels under Carlyon. "You know, Henry, that you always have my support." What else could he say? The burden was not his. If Carlyon's chalice was still foaming, it seemed to Martin that it was a poisoned one.

They fell silent, each brooding and locked into his own version of life, duty and the past, trying to make sense of it. At the very last moment of the evening, just before they had heard the stables clock strike eleven, and they heard the housekeeper's husband trudging down the corridors to complete the lock-up routine, Henry said, "You know, I can't help but have doubts about that boy." He continued in the silence, almost to himself, as Martin automatically stood up. "You see, I've been a farmer all my life. I could swear that boy was not full term when he was born. Yet he was supposed to have been three weeks late, and she absolutely refused to be induced. Yet he was a good weight. But I've never been able to take to him, even though he is my only son. Am I so wrong?"

Martin had known for thirteen years that this moment would come, and his reaction was well rehearsed. "Well," he said, "John is young yet. There is plenty of time. There goes the clock. I must away, before I get locked in too."

* * *

Chapter Eleven

Stone walls do not a prison make,
Nor iron bars a cage.
Minds innocent and quiet take
That for an hermitage.

Richard Lovelace

Monday March the twenty-seventh

Hetty was reading all about Mr Gwarior in the Camwul Echo. As the High Sheriff, he was representing the Queen and doing a lovely job. Mr Gwarior was such a handsome chap, with lovely silver hair and a really good suit. Funny how people turned out. Hetty remembered him and his cousin Martin with their air guns, terrifying the village, shooting magpies. Then, it was crossbows and seagulls, but that was criminal. They should a gone to prison. Nowadays, Henry had his pheasants and was giving out the prizes at the school fêtes to the conservationists. Funny how some bad boys grew up to be prominent citizens. 'Course, that was if they had the background to start with.

* * *

On Monday morning at nine, Jake sat on a smelly, worm-eaten nineteenth century desk that had been set up in the old schoolroom on the second floor in the north-facing wing. The room was cold and draughty. There was brown paper in the cracks where wood should have been in the windows. Bodruggan told him not to lean against any of the iron bars on the windows in case the whole lot fell out on to the terrace. What a drag. Still, anything was better than going back to school: not that there was a school in the west country that would take him.

Jake was not sure quite what he was expecting, but what came through the door reminded him of an escaped prep school teacher, with worn leather patches on a tweed jacket and a bow tie over an old fashioned shirt with a high, plastic collar. What a wanker. Jake stuck out his chin.

The wanker took a seat at the teacher's desk. They sized up one another. Neither of them said good morning. Jake continued to kick his heels against the legs of the desk.

After a while, the teacher unrolled a copy of the TES and started to read the front page. "So, what would you like to read? This is my comic: what's yours?"

"Read?"

The tutor put down his comic. "You do read?"

"Yes, very well, actually."

"Well, let's read. It will pass the time."

"There's nothing to read in here. Anyway, aren't you paid to teach me?"

"We won't talk about payment."

Jake looked around for a book. Eventually, he sorted through some pathetic old volumes on a dusty brown shelf and brought a fat pale green one with spongy pages up to the tutor's desk.

The man in the stupid bow tie looked up. "Do you want to read this Hobson's? It's a little out of date. Science has moved on since then. I can get you some better books than that. Hawkins' history of time is good. Do you know it?"

"I don't want to read it, anyway."

"I don't blame you. What would you like to do?"

"I don't want to read."

The tutor bent to his comic.

Jake said, "Might we go out?"

"What's the weather like?"

"Don't know." Jake shrugged his shoulders and looked vague.

"Have a look."

Jake went to the window. The tops of the fir trees were swaying about. "A bit rainy, but all right."

"What are the clouds doing?"

"Dunno. It's just grey. I don't know what they're doing. They're clouds, aren't they."

"Where's the wind?"

"Where?"

"In the east? In the north?"

"Well, I don't know, do I ?"

The tutor went to the window.

"Don't lean against it, sir. It could fall out."

The tutor looked grateful. "Thank you, John, I was about to try and open it."

"It won't open. Best not to try any of the windows on this floor. Call me Jake, not John."

"Call me Ishmael."

"Fishmeal?"

"I am Ahab, but call me Ishmael."

"I am John, but call me Jake."

They looked at each other. Nobody smiled.

"The wind is in the west, a steady four or five. It will be like this all day. We can dodge the showers. There is no heating in here, but the window glass feels quite warm. We're still in an Atlantic depression. It will be wet under foot. Collect your wellingtons and raincoat. Meet me by the front door. I'll show you how to read the weather."

The tutor went out of the schoolroom. Jake looked at the closed, snot-green door before going downstairs to fetch his Barbour and boots.

The tutor strode quickly along the terrace and down the steps towards the park, with John trailing after him. After admiring a cracked old urn, the young man said, "Well, you lead the way. What shall we look at?"

"Look at?"

"There must be plenty to look at here. Lots of interesting things. It's a bit late in the day to collect field mushrooms, they'll be wormy by now, but we could find out where they are coming up. Then we'll always have something to eat."

"There's plenty of food in the fridges." John turned up his nose. "There's plenty of dried mushroom Cuppasoup in the cupboards."

"There's sufficient food in the park to feed us, without loading up in a supermarket."

"We've got loads of tinned mushroom soup. And there's always a dozen mushroom-topped pizzas in the freezer."

After wandering about, looking at a starving hedgehog and a dead bird with large, jagged beak marks in it, Jake wanted to sit down on a great tree stump. The tutor sat down with him, staring at the sky, reading the weather.

"Have you come far?" Jake asked. "I mean, where are you from?"

"Oh, here and there."

"Yes but... What did you do before?"

"I'm a jobbing tutor."

"What's that?"

"I take jobs as a tutor."

"Cool. Ideal."

"Can be. Not always. I like novelty. Hello, what's this beauty? This is an odd season for you to be wandering about. How on earth did you survive the winter like this? You can't be this year's, can you?" A large, revolting, brown caterpillar was crawling about and rearing up on the tutor's hand. "He was in the plantain, eating like a horse. Pick some more plantain. He should be ready to pupate soon. He'll stop eating and start climbing before long. We'll take him into the house. I spotted some museum glass cases in the schoolroom. We'll use one of them. That'll liven things up. We've captured our first miracle, Jake. Come on."

Excited, the tutor went striding off across the park.

"I don't know what plantain is. Oh for fuck's sake." Jake trailed after him in the long grass.

* * *

Nothing much had been going on, down the beach, for some time, though it was the Easter holidays. Hetty dozed off a bit and thought about life. When she woke up, it was time for tea and her first thought was the kettle. She took up her binoculars automatically and was thrilled to see something entirely new. She seen Jack's boy, Ronnie, who was a fully qualified engineer and couldn't get no job since Holman's down Camborne closed its doors: she seen Ronnie drag a flabby white man on to the sand. She thought it was a fight at first, but then she remembered that Ronnie was a fully qualified lifeguard and was struggling with a bottle and a mask as thirty more people splashed into the water. Hetty didn't need no tide table. This was rip-tide time. She saw thirty people swept a hundred yard out to sea as if by magic. That was some rip-tide, that was.

"Go on, go on," she shouted to the stupid lifeguards who were dawdling about. Even from here, Hetty felt she could hear the people shouting, screaming, waving and drowning. Hetty unwrapped another bickie. After a minute or so, a dozen lifeguards started snatching jetskis and rescue boards and rescue floats. The rescue boat got underway somehow and the drowning crowds were scooped up out of the water as sixty more bathers were dashing out into the great luminous sea.

Hetty knew when the rip tide was over. She got down off the tallboy, went to the kitchen and stared up at the shale and heather cliff, and up to the ruin of Great Stack. She wondered what it would be like to go paddling now, with the sand being ripped out from under her toes. She remembered how her brother Jack used to hang his small striped towel that Mother bought him in Woolworth's, right over the sign that said, "Danger Falling Rock", and how he used to laugh. She could see him now. Jack broke his neck, diving off a rock into Low Pool. Jack was never no good no more after that, and was dead in a couple of years.

* * *

When Dingo had turned up at Irene's ex-council house on the hill with a 1969 blue Triumph motorbike and stripped it down in the front room on a piece of tarpaulin, Irene said nothing about it, because at least Dingo was home with her again, eating her lardy cake and drinking her lager. She hadn't asked about it, and he didn't say anything, but perhaps he was going into business again. She wanted to encourage that. It seemed like the old days, when she and Mike were first married and Mike was on contract in the mine and they lived in poverty together, before the children came along. Dingo didn't mind being fed proper meals. He still didn't drink tea, but in the evenings they could go to the pub together and come home together. He was able to wear a few of Mike's bigger shirts, which she still kept in the drawer. She bought him some new trousers and got him a tweed jacket from one of the better charity shops in town. He looked quite respectable; she thought that he might stay that way, until the day the bike was finished: and then he was off again, back to his caravan by the road. She was getting fed up with being exploited like this.

* * *

After doing some stupid pond-dipping, Jake said to Ishmael, "Let's go down to the folly."

"Folly? I didn't know there was a folly at Carlyon."

"That's because it's grown over and can't be seen from the house. My friend lives there."

"Lives there?"

Jake led the way through the rhododendron and small trees. "Look, here it is. Isn't it fine? It's got a terrific fireplace and winding stair up to battlements. I'll show you. Daddy and Uncle Martin used to play war games here. Mr Bodruggan's never far away. He's the head gardener here. Have you met him? Everyone knows Mr Bodruggan. Mummy hates him but Daddy says he has to stay and can't be sacked. Not now, not ever."

The tutor looked into the distance. "What it must be to have a permanent place," he said, "where one can never be sacked. What sort of place is that?"

"Carlyon's a fine place. Anyway, you'd get bored here. You like moving on, you said. You're a jobbing tutor, remember?"

"Every jobbing tutor is looking for a permanent fine place; not just somewhere to stay for a while."

They looked for Bodruggan, but he was out and the door was open. They went in.

"My goodness. That's a Henry Cleere."

"Yes I know. How did you know that? Do you like fireplaces?"

"What's it doing in a folly, Jake? Look at the fine marble, the way the sculptor has worked with the stone. This is breathtaking. Look at the detail. Notice the little carved feet. This is very rare. A very fine example."

"Yes I know. It's Victorian."

"No, it's older. It belongs in a great house. Does your father know there is a fireplace of this quality in a folly in the grounds? Look at the figures carved in the marble panels."

"Of course he does, but he doesn't ever come here. Mr Bodruggan looks after the folly for Daddy. You see, during the Civil War, the Bodruggans had no-where to go. The fireplace came here with them, after a while, that is. The story is that this was a woodsman's thatched stone cottage in the grounds, before my great grandfather built the folly. When their house was sacked, the fireplace was all that was left. Bodruggan says they brought it here.

Bodruggan says they are sentimental about the fireplace. They had to lie low for a generation or two."

"No, the fireplace isn't Civil War."

"Anyway, Mr. Bodruggan's not here. Let's go back to the house for tea. I'm fed up with being outside. It's wet. Can't we do some reading now?"

They left the folly and walked outside into the gloom under the wet trees. They were gathering up their pond-dipping nets and jars in the twilight when they heard a noise. Bodruggan was standing in the doorway, holding a storm lantern.

"Now then Master John," he said. "Now then, Tutor. Time to be off." He shut the door briskly, leaving them in darkness.

"That's very strange," said Ishmael. "How did he get back into the folly?"

"Oh, Bodruggan's weird like that. He was probably up in the battlements all the time."

"Why didn't he answer when you called to him?"

"I don't know, do I? The Bodruggans are very cautious."

"You mean there are more of them?"

"Daddy says, that's the way it is with the Bodruggans."

"Oh."

"Since the Civil War."

"Residing in a folly?"

"It really was the Bodruggans' fireplace originally. Daddy says it's sin by Osis between Carlyon and the

Bodruggans, whatever that means. Do you know what it means?"

"Not unless I have the context, no."

* * *

Chapter Twelve

I won't make you sad, there'll be no tears in going,
Won't you roll me in your arms,
Just remember me with smiles, always keep the laughter flowing

(sung by The Cromer Smugglers)

April the sixteenth: Easter Sunday

Kevin and Darren had been up Margaret's shop to do their shopping early. Whilst Margaret was on the 'phone to the police about them, they got a pile of 'phone cards.

Then, coming out smartly and round the corner, they fell into the fists of some small, pale, thin foreigners they recognised as the daffodil pickers who were up Hope Farm. Before they had a chance to ask what the wages were up there, they realised they'd been robbed. It didn't matter. They didn't have a phone. They retreated to the safety of their bus shelter.

Darren and Kevin stared at the bus as it came to a standstill. Nobody got off and nobody got on. The driver sat with the doors open, staring out at the hot tarmac, baking behind his toughened glass screen. If the weather continued hot like this, it was going to be a hell of a summer. And he did not see why he had to work on a Bank Holiday, when everybody stayed at home and nobody took a bus to anywhere.

After a minute, the driver looked at this watch. He unhooked himself and got out of his pen. He walked to the back of the bus with a bin liner and scooped up some of the detritus on the floor and on the seats. He chucked the bin liner into the drain beside the road. Kevin and Darren were aghast and were outraged at the idea of a bus driver dumping litter in the drain, but they stayed cool.

Suddenly, the driver snatched up a book that was left on a seat. He went to the platform and threw the book out. It landed in the bus shelter, where Kevin and Darren were pointedly staring up and down the road.

A gull started squawking on Old Pard's cold chimney.

"No need for that," Darren said, offended.

Kevin thought further and said, after a while, "'Ee thinks we's older than we really is."

Darren absorbed the idea and looked at the white book that had shells on the front: or pictures of them, anyhow. He moved over and picked it up.

"Is a cookery book," he said. "That Rick Stein up Padsta." He dropped it.

Kevin took it up, after a while. He opened up to page sixty-nine. Slowly, he read, "A fish filleting knife, a blade that is about 7 inches (18 cm) and flexible, made either of carbon steel, which is easy to sharpen but hard to keep clean, such as a Victorin... or Gus..." And he read, "An extra large cook's knife with a 10-inch (25 cm) blade for cutting lob... and craw... in half."

Kevin looked up at the cracked chimney pot, where the sandwich gull was making that dry laughing sound, that low cackling noise they sometimes make when they are observing mankind. He thought about the ten inch blade and the extra large cook who fed him chips and hot pie, up school. Suddenly, his guts burned for school.

"Darr...," he said, "Shallus get on the bus one day? Got any change for the bus, 'ave 'ee?"

"No," Darren said, suspiciously. "I ebn' got no change for no bus, an' you ebn' neither. So don' even think about ut. We got a place to go to, an' thas 'ere. Think a they poor buggers that robbed us of our phone cards. They only got a tent."

* * *

This time, she didn't hesitate. After a couple of days had passed, Irene walked down to fetch Dingo. This time, she believed that she had earned the right to fetch him home with her. Anyway, she had a letter for him from his probation officer. She didn't need to read his letters because he had learned to read very well in the prison, but somehow she felt the need to read them anyway. This was a good letter because it was all about Dingo having to get a proper address, because he couldn't live in an abandoned workman's caravan beside a by-pass. That was no address. Either he would have to move in with Irene or, reluctantly, the probation officer would have to recommend that he went back to prison.

The weather had closed in by the time she turned off the by-pass and threaded her way through the heather to Dingo's caravan. For a moment, she thought he wasn't there. Then she thought she would have to shout to get his attention because the compound he had built around himself with wire netting was locked up with a big Squire padlock. But he'd already seen her coming and let her in without a word and without looking at her. It was a grudging welcome.

"What've you done with yer bike?" She said, for something to say.

"Gone. Got rid of 'n."

Irene thought he meant that he had sold the bike for profit. It so, this was good news. She bucked up considerably and felt the future swell.

Irene unwrapped the pasty with its hard, pale pastry. Immediately, an aroma of kitchens and women who work in the home filled the tiny space in the caravan. Dingo bowed his head.

"You didn' 'ave to," he said. "I rather you didn'."

Irene sighed and looked about. "Well, Saturday's my day for making them, holiday time'r no. I made one for everybody. I went to work until twelve an' then come 'ome and made one each fer the boys. This is yesterday's. I warmed un up again for 'ee." She watched a spider let itself down from the roof on to the damp army blankets and sacking. "You don't 'ave to live 's poor as this. You got a 'ome to go to. You bein' there won't affect my money, you know."

The bright lie was absorbed in the gloom. After a while, Dingo began to eat. He ate cautiously, as though his teeth needed fixing. He ate slowly, looking at the food carefully, both hands around the still warm pasty.

"Will 'ee come home this evening," she said. "For a lager an' a warm-up? I got the fire goin' with your oily rags. Is not smokin'."

"Best to get going," he said. "Get dark soon." He went on eating. "I'll take 'ee to the road. You'll tear up yer stockens, otherwise."

They drank a few beers and talked and laughed about the old days in Coen parish, the characters they had known and the things that used to go on, before their time: Jimmy Veal's pony and trap; Dingo's father's old cob, who was called Rob and who used to look back to see who was driving; the incendiary bomb that Mary Allen's mother found in the field. Through it all, Dingo seemed distracted and Irene didn't want to intrude too far, so she kept it going, the reminiscing and the scandalising and the gossiping. Too late in the evening, she told him she wanted him to go home with her, because she could never sleep here. There was no room for her, and she feared for his safety. She told him so. The place was damp and there was bad boys around now. Had he heard about Old Pard's place? What they done up there? And that 'ouse is in the middle of the village. You would think somebody would a seen somethin' gwoin' on. If they done that there, what would they do 'ere, when nobody was lookin', an' there was nobody to call out to, in this lonely place, eh? An' what did that probation officer say in 'is letter? That Dingo had to get a job an' a proper place to stay or 'ee'd 'ave'n back in the prison. He was only out on licence, so 'ee could be brought back any time, don't forget. An' you couldn' argue with the law.

175

"Tomorrow is Metanoia," Dingo said.

No, never. That was Christmastime, wasn't it? They already had Lent, and this was Easter Sunday: but she didn't contradict him. She was no church-goer.

At last, it was time to go. They said nothing about it, but Irene felt that they had reached an ending, some kind of ending; not Advent, not a new waiting for a new birth. There were no new births on her horizon. It was too late for that. Not at her time of life. Half of her was ready to crack a new joke, but she didn't want to refer to it, in case it was all in her imagination, and she thought that things would go on the same if she said nothing. Dingo would go to church, have a drink in the Steam Engine across the Round and go on up the hill to her place, sit in the porch with the paper and his *Great Expectations* book and look at the sea through the glass. Ambrose's grandson, Barry's boy next door would be back from his eleven days' fishing up Greenland out of Hull with the Lemares. They would have a few beers and a laugh about the seasickness and the bleeding hands and the Vaselene and the iceberg and the icy acres and the Spanish vessels and the greet German factory ship and the Icelanders and the helicopters buzzing around and the skipper that never slept and the Polish engineer an' the...

Rain had ceased. The sky was pale and the innocent moon was up, to light Irene home when she left Dingo at the roadside. All was silent whilst water dripped into the earth from the vegetation. There was no more for her to do. The warm Playing Place lights were winking orange and yellow, a mile away.

"Do 'ee remember how it used to be s'dark up the Playin' Place? When you stepped outside the Steam Engine, there was just a few lights. Gruzelier's lamp light in the kitchen an' the Vicar's light in his study an' Ronald Bonnin'ton's movin' blue light from 'is television. An' that was about it, wadna? Now the place is lit up like Falmouth Docks. Ol' orange lights all over, an' all they bungalow lights, an' all they estates gwoin up, even up top the cliffs. Remember 'ow dark it was up there on the cliffs, they days?"

Dingo swallowed and suppressed his cough, his tartan scarf over his mouth; but she did not fail to notice that he had been wheezing as she followed him through the heather.

"Come down the pub later," she said.

"I'll watch 'ee down the road."

"Did 'ee see that fallin' star?" Irene said.

Dingo thought of the happy boy who flew too close to the sun, in his wings of beeswax and feathers. He thought of how the jealous god destroyed the boy with a sunbeam, and of how his father could do nothing other than to watch. He thought of the pale legs sliding into the green water that would have felt like concrete. They sleep with the fishes, he said to himself, all of them, Wally and Peter and ten thousand more, out there in Coen Bay, where there was no surf, just green water.

"Thas Icarus up there," he said.

"No, thas the Plough. You forgot the stars. You bin in prison too long."

"Now you wan' put me back there, one way or 'nother."

"Don' 'ee be s' daft, Dingo. Is just, you ebm got nowhere t' go to."

She hesitated, turned and went on. She wanted to say something more, about always having a place to stay with her, because that was love: but meaning was lost, somehow, in this brooding night.

By the time she reached the cross-roads on the downs, Dingo saw that the darkness had closed around her. Arthur Bodruggan's voice, which had been held back whilst Irene was chattering in front of him, now returned; and it kept echoing in and out of his mind: "Time to go now, Dingo. I think is time, don't you? Time to go, Dingo. Thas it, ol' Dingo, time to go now."

When at the cross-roads she turned back to wave, Dingo's form was no longer visible in the gloom. He must have thought she wouldn't be bothered to turn back and wave her hand to him: but she would, she would always bother.

Still, she was carrying his dirty vest and his pants to wash. That was something. And she would take him a pillowslip and a sheet to change next time. And a bottle of Veno's. That was something to look forward to.

* * *

"Ishmael?" Jake looked up from his nineteenth century entomology textbook, where he was copying a very good line drawing of a mosquito, even though it was

Sunday. He preferred to be up here with the specimen cases and the tutor. It didn't matter what day it was. At least he wasn't in church with his awful parents.

The jobbing tutor looked up from the bulging green supplement in his TES comic.

"Yah?"

"Which is the deadliest of all the species?"

The tutor looked back to the picture of an American telecommunications expert being beheaded by a religious fanatic on television.

"Mankind. By a long chalk. Keep your distance. Always stand by the door."

Jake put down his textbook and looked across the desk at the tutor sitting by the door, who looked across at Jake, sitting by the window.

* * *

Still trembling, Old Pard's sister telephoned the last number in the Yellow Pages. Emergency freephone-callout:

"I want fer you to come and put a launder back on my place, thas falled down. I knaw is Easter Sunday, but somebody's bin an' robbed my place of all my money an' stood on the launder to git in th'attic while I was in church, and the slates on the roof is probably broak too, but we shent knaw until it d'rain. I want the launder put back, any'ow, right away. Is emergency."

There was a pause. "I don't know what a launder is."

"You are a builder, aren'tee?" Old Pard's sister sat in the bentwood chair for a very long time, staring out at the raked-over, yellow mining plain that was scheduled to become America's greatest garbage dump in Europe. She wondered if she had already died and had gone to one of they parallel universes.

* * *

A gipsy caravan was already parked on the side of the verge by Billy Bray's chapel when they got there to the bus-stop in the late morning with a bag of smoky bacon crisps from Margaret's. Darren and Kevin watched as a woman in a red headscarf got out of the caravan and put out a sign saying, "Cornish Pat Fortune Telling." They watched her go back inside. She never came out all day. Not even for a piss. Nobody went inside. This wasn't really a tourist village. Not yet, anyhow. It wasn't cold, but it was raining all day. It had been raining nearly all week.

At eight o'clock, when the boys were thinking perhaps she had sneaked out the back or something, a removal van appeared and parked in the mud. The gipsy caravan was put on a trailer on the back. The woman got in beside the driver and they drove off.

They never saw it in Hellick village again. So, what was all that about?

* * *

Chapter Thirteen

And comes that other fall we name the fall.
He says the highway dust is over all

Robert Frost: The Oven Bird

April the seventeenth. Easter Day

It was Easter Morning at Carlyon. It was the fourth day of rain, but this was the morning for coloured eggs, and Mrs Sawle had spent the early hours of the morning dyeing the shells in different saucepans on the Aga before she went off to her sister's funeral up in Brighton, where poor Ada had drowned herself, some weeks before, in February.

Christice chose a bright yellow egg. Henry chose a blue egg that had turned grey. Jake snatched up a blotchy red one which had gone brown again in the pan. The tutor was left with the small pinkish one.

Because Mrs Sawle was not there to lay the table, there was some difficulty with spoons and knives. Henry became irritated because everybody kept getting up and opening and shutting drawers in the sideboard. Then, no-one wanted to get up from the table and go down the long corridor, through the green baize door which was now a fire-door, through the old butler's parlour, through the kitchens, through the preparation rooms to the scullery, where there was some butter in a fridge. Then there was a difficulty about the marmalade. Jake emptied the crystal jar, licked the silver spoon and placed the sticky jar on the heavy white damask table cloth in front of Henry. This caused Henry to shuffle about silently. He stared at the ceiling in agony. At last, Christice went out towards the kitchen. There was an unconscionable delay whilst Christice filled the jar in the pantry and returned with it. There followed the problem of the licked spoon, which could not be used again. Christice thought there might be another small silver spoon in a sideboard drawer, which normally lived in a mustard pot; but when it was found, it was seen to be tarnished and did not reach to the bottom of the old Waterford crystal jar; so it fell into the marmalade and could only be retrieved by somebody putting their fingers down through the neck of the jar. At this point, everybody gave up with marmalade, except for Jake, who licked the second spoon and wiped his fingers surreptitiously on the hem of the damask cloth under the table, where nobody noticed the sticky smear until the next meal.

During breakfast, the sun made a brief appearance. Christice sat with the sun in her eyes, making a frightful mess of her egg. There was yoke down the yellow chicken-moulded eggcup, with shells littering the saucer. Laying down his *Telegraph* newspaper momentarily, Henry picked small pieces off the top of his egg, before lining up his knife and slicing off the crown with precision, catching it neatly in his spoon. He stared furiously at Jake, who was holding his egg spoon at the tip of the handle and bashing at one side of his egg. The tutor sat bolt upright, a little apart, chewing neatly.

Henry said, "It's unseasonably warm outside, I feel. This rain is a trial. With the wind in the south, the rain clouds seem to form over our heads deliberately in order to bucket over Carn Keen every morning and afternoon. Everything is waterlogged. The ground is sodden. They can't get the machinery out onto the land. Everything is held up."

"Well it's quite nice outside now, Henry. In fact, the sun is in my eyes. Close the curtain a bit. Haven't you noticed, the sun is out now? It's been out for five minutes at least. I can't see a thing here."

Henry rustled the paper. "I see that General Sir Rory Basset-Gore has died at the ripe old age of ninety-two. Fell asleep watching the sunset in his rocking-chair on his porch in Cape Town, where he spent his last years. Of course, the Cornish gentry were a warrior race. We especially. We even have it in our name, don't we. Gwarior. Ever warriors, throughout the ages. Standard bearers to William the Conqueror and all that."

Christice addressed the empty end of the table. "Actually, Gwarior means "player" in the Cornish language, which doesn't suggest a Norman family to me; and Carlyon was snatched from the Carlyons, of whom I am one, in a game of spoof, if you happen to remember. At least, that's what it says in Banister-Cowper. Perhaps Banister-Cowper isn't a reliable historian. Is Banister-Cowper reliable, do you think?"

Before anybody could frame a reply, she turned her blonde head to her son. "I don't understand what you were doing with the bicycle and the ticker-tape yesterday

183

afternoon, John. You seemed to be just peddling about on your bicycle. You didn't seem to be doing anything useful. Mr Ishmael, you were standing about with a pencil and paper for over an hour in the fog. I don't understand what you were doing all that time in the mizzle. Were you doing something? Shouldn't you have been in the schoolroom doing sums or something, if you were not going to church? We agreed you didn't have to go to church, provided you were reading something religious in the schoolroom."

"We were studying Newton's Christian Laws of Motion, Mummy. The Newtonian world was a clockwork edifice until Einstein came along."

There was an awkward silence.

Henry grunted. "He's making a fearful mess of his egg. Can't you teach him how to eat?" The spoon having finally penetrated the shell with some force, egg yolk was now spattered far and wide, down the eggcup, over the chequered top tablecloth and the yellow, furry Cockerel egg-cosy.

"He's only a little boy. Aren't you, darling? Eat up your eggy-weg. Stop being a bully, Henry. My plate is just as messy as his."

"Quite."

One by one, the family stopped eating and peered down the table at the silent tutor's place below the salt and pepper. There was a smear of butter on his knife and a few crumbs on his side plate, where his soldiers had been. His egg spoon showed some modest signs of recent use. His eggcup was shining clean. There was no sign of the dyed pink shell anywhere. Cross legged, sitting at a slight angle to the table, he was sipping his coffee with a hand for the cup and a hand for the saucer, clearly thinking about something else.

When they got away to the schoolroom, Jake said, "Typical you. How did you manage that?"

The tutor thought a moment.

"I'll show you how to blow an egg and lacquer a Japanese scene on it, if you like. Then I think I must pack."

"Going somewhere?"

"I'd like to get away before the next cloudburst."

They spent a productive morning in the schoolroom and watched huge cloud formations build up, almost directly above them. Taking a break from concentrated painting with tiny brushes, they went to the window. The tutor remarked that there was much energy in the weather today: enormous energy, in fact. This was a result of all this unseasonable heat, in the south. One could see how warm air from the south was coming on to the land, meeting the colder onshore winds from the north, which were sliding under, and how the whole thing was billowing upwards. They tapped the schoolroom barometer several times. Laden with moisture, cold air was being sucked in off the sea, on the other side of the coast, being driven upwards to thirty thousand feet, ready to condense.

* * *

It was not unusual for Shaun Mee to take a day off work, take the bus to Camwul, have a few jars in town and walk back to the parish, if the weather was not too bad. He didn't think it was right that he had to work a half day on Easter Day.

He'd already had a bit of a row with old man Bodruggan about poor time-keeping, so he thought that the best thing to do was not to turn up to work at all, if it meant getting another bollocking from the old fart. He was fed up with it. He shouldn't be at work, it was Easter, anyhow. A lot of men in his position, with a bad leg and a damaged spine, wouldn't go to work. He had the right to claim benefit for the rest of his life, but well, he wasn't lazy. He liked to go to work sometimes. They paid quite well, up Carlyon. His compensation money didn't last long, so he had to go to work, really, and there were very few jobs close to home. Just as well Rob Moon broke his back years ago because Rob Moon was out of work now, since the pumps were turned off at Wheal Cuckoo. So who was the lucky one with the safe job?

Luck was like that, Mee thought. Luck went in lumps. Sometimes you had a great lump of luck chucked at you, and then sometimes you had it taken out of you in gert lumps. Today, for instance, he'd fed the Pot of Gold machine from eleven in the morning until two in the afternoon. A lot of coins went in; then a lot of coins suddenly cascaded out. Then they all went back in again, one by one. Then it was all over and he was broke.

Slipping away from the Crow Bar, he leaned against the wall and held his breath for a few seconds, so that his head could clear. Then he started the long, slow, draggy climb through Camwul town, past the charity shops and the pubs and the slaughterhouse, where the pigs were normally giving it welly, but it was quiet today, being Easter. Up the hill, he came upon a rotten gang of kids, hanging around outside Tregeagle Park, sprawled out on the steps of the first world war monument. They demanded money and then started throwing rocks at him. Luckily, he was able to chuck his empty wallet at them before escaping into Charlie Mayne's old saddlery buildings. He got out the other side and slipped through the back lanes of terraced houses on the hill, on through the Roadway Fields and up on to the granite plain. There, he felt free again. He heard Camwul town clock chime three, and looked back at the bilious town, glistening in the watery sunlight. Fore Street looked like a slug trail, he thought. He found a dry rock to sit on and opened up his take-away brandy bottle. This was the best time of the day.

After a while, the rain came in again, sweeping down over the hillside. He thought he ought to get moving. His bad leg started to hurt a bit, and his muscles that supported the twist in his spine started their insistent ache. He fished a couple of pills out of his back pocket and downed them with the last of the spirit. Then he limped off, down the soggy path to the high moor.

He used to like the moors and the downs, all the wild places that were fast being tamed. You used to be able to stand on Carn Keen and look down on all the shafts, great penny circles in the landscape, with walls built around them. First they knocked down the engine houses and the stamps and took away the pumping machinery. That was before his time. But then you could see that they weren't going to stop there. De Gras built the great dam and the big white concrete block offices. Before long, Manpower Services were planting fir trees on the downs, taking away the avenues of spoil that told you where you were, ripping up medieval field systems, the archaeologist said. Mee knew that because he worked for the Manpower Services people for a while, before he started work up at Carlyon. Then they started capping the shafts. They couldn't leave it alone, could they? Anything to create jobs. Finally, Gwarior, the plonker, leased it to the council. And now it was fast on its way to becoming the biggest garbage dump in Europe. The latest was, they would be importing garbage from America to fill it. But then somebody told them that was all wrong, because American garbage was different from Cornish garbage and would destroy the environment, if all the muck seeped down: which of course it would, mining ground being the most drained ground he could think of. The whole bleddy parish was a drain, underground. Everybody knew that. Except them.

When the rain started to pour, Shaun Mee thought, oh hell, he'd left his jacket in the Crow Bar and it was too late to go back for it now. Well, never mind. He sheltered under a thorn tree that was leaning sideways out of a habit of the wind, rolled a spliff and thought about how long it would take to get across the Roadway Fields, which was a bit exposed, with no shelter he could think of, not even a thorn tree, except for the hedge, if the weather got really bad and cold.

It looked as though the rain was not going to give up, so after a quarter of an hour of getting damp feet, Shaun Mee thought, sod it, he'd better just plod on a bit. After a while, he saw the new by-pass in the distance, cut through the landscape like a great wound, where there was once a little ribbon of a road that wound past Dingo's scrap yard, and he headed for that. Why did they have to build everything so big and fat? Still, never mind. One good thing about the by-pass was that it was long and straight and would take him straight home.

* * *

When the rain began to fall, the daffodil pickers refused to eat their dog food and refused to go out, for the last time. Not even when they found themselves staring down the barrel of a shotgun would they move from their sodden, flooded tents.

In any case, the yellow daffodils had long since stopped nodding in the breeze. They were all drooping into the mud that had once been a field.

As the foreigners were ushered into the church rescue bus by Robert Morley Jones and Mrs Georgina Dartsby, they were pleased to see that parts of the field were moving down the hillside in fierce little rivulets. They were glad to say good-bye to the cold, alien fields where they were lucky not to have died of exposure.

* * *

Jake held back his tears when he saw the Tutor's taxi go down the long wet drive and disappear around the bend. He did not rush out to say good bye, as he used to do when people were fired by Mummy. There was no point. Jake heard Christice firing Ishmael on the spot just a few minutes after Ishmael went down to resign, for failing to follow the National Curriculum, something which she had just heard about on the radio. The Tutor put up a good defence for a liberal education, but the poor man was defeated by Mummy's alco-logic. So that was the end of the Tutor.

Jake went up to the schoolroom for the last time and peered in at the glass case, where Flubbs lay curled up in his leathery jacket amongst the rotted plantain leaves. He liked to think that Flubbs was sleeping amongst the brown stalks, but he knew from all the Tutor's careful scientific reasoning that the caterpillar was now in its chrysalis form, with its decaying vegetation wrapped around it. He knew that inside, Flubbs was a soup of molecules, and that sometime soon, this Summer, a miracle might happen. Flubbs might emerge as a beautiful hawk moth. Or he might not make it, because Flubbs ought to have gone to sleep in the Autumn, not in the Spring. There was a good chance of survival, but it would depend on all sorts of environmental conditions, and on the quality and strength of the chrysalis itself.

Jake removed the heavy top of the glass case. Going to the jammed window, he poked out all of the flimsy picture-glass panes, clearing away the thin shards into a neat pile in the corner, so that Flubbs would have every chance of escape, at the moment when he was ready. Then Jake glanced up at the sky to read the weather, thinking, gosh, huge banks of clouds were still boiling up, so he might go down with one of the men and cover up the horses before the rain really came down. Taking down the set of new encyclopaedias, Jake quickly looked up the tutor's names: Ahab, the king and Ishmael, son of Hagar. 'His hand will be against every man, and every man's hand against him.' He smiled about the disappearing eggshell trick, looked up proudly at his row of lacquered eggs and felt all right about the jobbing tutor moving on. Then he closed the door on Carlyon's schoolroom.

As he nipped down the back stairs, a plan began to form in Jake's mind that he would rather like to seem to go to school with Darren and Kevin in Keen Comprehensive School. That way, he could bunk off most days, like they did. Anyway, they seemed like chaps who knew how to have a jolly good time. He rather hoped that he might be able to travel in the back of a school bus. That would be a novelty.

On the way to the paddock, he met Rosudgeon, who was fiddling about with a rake in the rain. The sky was black, the clouds churning very fast. Looking up at Carn Keen, he saw lightening strike the television mast.

He shouted against the wind.

"Where's Bodruggan?"

"You ought not to be out in the wet with no coat on, John. You should git back in th' 'ouse."

"I want to get the horses in."

"Bodruggan's busy. Can't be asked. Not at this time."

"Look at the sky, will you? I've got to get the horses in."

"Yeah but Bodruggan's busy, John."

They were beginning to shout at each other as heavy drops of rain began to fall on them. Rosudgeon looked up at the carn. The rain was closing in. There was darkness over the moor. Wind was scything in from the sea, tearing at their clothes.

Rosudgeon looked as though he did not know what to do.

"The horses will bolt. They'll be struck by lightening. We've got to get them in, Mr Rosudgeon."

Rosudgeon looked at the direction of the churning ocean and then at the carn, where rain was bucketing down. The part-time gardener saw water flowing down the hillside in huge rivulets, taking clods of heather down with it. Some of the smaller boulders were beginning to move.

"'Ee's in the folly, but don't you say I said so."

Then they were both stumbling and running down towards the folly, as stair-rods of water came down on them. Water was running off the sodden lawns into the drains, which were becoming blocked with debris before their eyes. Manhole covers were up and spouting. Thrashing through the rhododendron, they came to the folly at last. There was no need to bang at the door. The door was open. Bodruggan was inside.

The carpet was thrown aside; the trap-hatch was up and Bogruggan was peering down into the fast flowing adit that went down to the sea, saying, "Bugger bugger bugger, oh bugger," his cap-lamp flashing on to the swirling black, rising underground tide.

"But we're safe, aren't we? The house is safe isn't it? We're a mile from the sea."

"We're at the top of the tide. The bleddy water is backin' up."

"What is?"

Without taking his eyes off the underground, Bodruggan shouted to Rosudgeon, "Open up the pond sluice. Dig out a channel for the water. Ease the water off, anywhere you see a build-up."

Rosudgeon seemed rooted, staring at the traphatch, listening to the water rushing underground.

"Git gwoin'. Git gwoin'. Give 'im a 'and, John."

Hearing the edge in Bodruggan's voice, Rosudgeon rushed out into the darkened landscape, looking all around him.

Jake stayed. "What is this traphatch? I've never seen this before. All the times I've come here, I never knew this existed. You've never shown this to me."

The old man stood up. He turned off his lamp. There was the roaring of the wind in the trees, and the roaring of the water underground. He pulled the heavy wooden cover over the square hole in the floor, to mask the sound of the torrent in the adit.

From the gloom, Arthur Bodruggan said, "This is the foundation of your House, son, which we kept gwoin' from the civil war on, yes, 'gainst all sorts, with whatever come to 'and... An' now I think you may 'ave los'un yet, through no fault of yer own. I tol' your father he had to go, an' now is come to this."

"What do you mean? What do you mean? The house is safe."

Not hurrying any more, Bodruggan walked out into the storm, to seek another shelter under the tallest solitary tree in the park.

The sound ceased underground as the water began to fill the shaft. There was an eerie stillness in the folly, which Jake did not comprehend.

* * *

Down at the bus stop, where the water was flowing past, down Railway Terrace, and Kevin and Darren were standing on the remains of their much carved bench, clinging to the side of the bus shelter, Darren called out to Kevin, "Shall us git on the next bus, 'en?"

Kevin looked all round, at the river at their feet and the drains bubbling up shit and paper. He glanced across at Old Pard's house, where they could have been staying, if the pigs and Kevin's brother hadn't chased them out and it hadn't been boarded up. He looked up at the rooks in the tall trees that somehow were unable to settle.

"Nah," he said. "Bus went stop 'ere no more. Not now, willuh."

They stayed where they were. They clung to the sides and waited for the waters to go down.

* * *

Old Joseph Hocking was in his chair in the attic, sitting under the skylight, when the rain came down. For a while, he listened to the changing tone of the rain on the glass as the sky darkened and the water began to drum on the slate on the roof. For a while longer, he was patient, and thought of other rains and other seasons, before he was driven to push himself, bit by bit, out of the way of the drips falling into his lap. By the time he had rocked himself and his chair to the wall of the room, he was already soaking wet and shouting for Michael's wife, Clem.

When he heard the yellow helicopters overhead, he wondered whether he would have to be moved, but then he thought, no, the Steam Engine was built on the Playing Place and the Playing Place was at the apex of all the good ground in the parish: apart from Carn Keen, which was something else. There must be some reason why the Playing Place was built where it was. The ancient ones must have known something. And there again, he'd never known any building around the Playing Place to flood. Mexico House and Montana House, they never flooded. They was built on good ground. The old vicarage, well that never flooded. A shaft went in once, in the vegetable garden. Frightened the vicar's wife out of her wits. Sides was swept clean. Cabbages was gone. But the vicarage was never flooded out. Dry as a bone. 'Cept for the walls. Always had damp walls. It was Gruzelier's fields that never drained. Funny that. Reclaimed mining ground, but the soil was clayey, for all that.   When 'e built they bungalows, Hocking told 'im, "That groun' do never drain." Mud everywhere when they was buildin' them. Told 'im so. Still, they sold 'em, every las' one of 'em. Eventually. An' where did Gruzelier end up to? In the vicarage Old People's Home. Bankrupt with his friend, Bridger the builder. Dead. All dead now. But Joseph was still alive. Funny, that. Joseph was still alive. Ambrose died in 'is own bed, and Joseph would die in 'is own bed. But 'ee would die in 'is own chair if Clem didn' come soon, because the water from the skylight was drippin' on to the floor and makin' 'un s'cold in 'ere.

When the lights went out, Joseph Hocking said well, this was bleddy redic'lous. But Clem soon came up with a bottle: a hot water bottle, which made Joseph annoyed. He made her go down and get a proper bottle of something.

She came back up with a step-ladder and had a go at fastening the skylight, but told him that the skylight was phucked and it needed somebody stronger than her to get it shut proper; but Michael was out in all this wind and rain, moving a beech tree that had fallen over across the yard.

After half a bottle, Joseph thought that it would be no great trouble to get out of the chair and get up on the step-ladder and fasten the hatches. For the first time in weeks, he threw his blanket off and tottered across to the stepladder, where he jammed himself against the side and pulled himself up with a pair of arms that were still bulldog strong from nearly a century of pulling beer barrels about in the cellar, taking his legs with him somehow.

Up at the top, he poked his head out of the skylight, thinking, well, it was quite rainy but invigorating in a sort of way. The brandy kept out the cold. He could see the helicopters now in the distance, where they were hovering about Maynard's Cove. He thought it would be quite nice to build a sort of Captain's walk up here. The planning people would never know. He could build a sort of Pepper Pot up here, or a sort of Lantern. He could start shouting "Heva heva" when he saw a shoal of fish out to sea. Come to that, he could shout any bleddy thing he liked, whether he saw fish or no.

After a while, when it was getting quite dark, though it must still have been the middle of the afternoon, he noticed a helicopter hovering over him and a man waving at him from the open cockpit door. It was very noisy and hellish windy, but sort of quiet at the same time, with the light going and the cold and wet getting quite numbing. He roped himself up to what he thought was a mast with his dressing-gown cord.

He was still singing "Nearer my God to Thee" when they plucked him and his empty brandy bottle from the skylight, where he had got his feet jammed up somehow in the collapsing step-ladder. In fact, when winchman Geoffrey Biggins got him hitched up to the harness, he realized that so tangled up was Joseph Hocking, they nearly took the step-ladder and the skylight with them as well. There had been nothing in Biggins' training to prepare him for such an eventuality, as he explained to his commanding officer in his debriefing.

* * *

It was heavier going than he ever thought it would be, but Shaun Mee finally made it to the by-pass. He was soaked through. His clothes were completely useless and he felt like pulling them off. They just seemed to weigh him down. Sometimes he felt he was walking on air, and he couldn't feel his fingers any more. He stamped and ran a bit. He was annoyed with himself for drinking so much spirits. He wasn't exactly drunk when he left town. He was quite lucid. He just wasn't up to blundering about in the wet like this, and he was sure he'd gone the wrong way round, sinking into mud and nearly losing a boot at one stage.

Now he reached the footings of the by-pass, he thought that he would climb up on to the road and hitch a lift, if he could. He hadn't seen any cars on the road for some time and wasn't surprised because the sky had gone black and the rain felt like sticks coming down on him: and painful they were too. Nobody would be driving about in this.

He got up to the bend in the road where he recognised Dingo's place. If he could get to Dingo's caravan, he could get inside and dry out. He wanted to see another human being's face.

He'd never thought about it before, but he suddenly realised that he was sinking into the boggy ground on the valley bottom. A lot of water was standing in the fields behind him, but worse than that, the Lannarth steam that went through the pathetically inadequate culvert in the road was blocked solid and backing up, with a lot of brown water, earth and debris that had tumbled down from the hillside. Vegetation had been pulled down by the water, with boulders and a soup made out of soil and earth. He would have to move away from where he stood and try to find another way of climbing up onto the road. He suddenly felt unsafe here.

He moved further along the valley, but even as he did, a wave of water lapped at his ankles. He turned around to find a pool of dirty water rising against the side of the road's embankment. Looking across the valley for an explanation, he saw that the angry, rushing stream was in spate. He found himself sinking, pulled his feet out quickly and ran stumbling for higher ground.

For a while, he clung to the side of the embankment of the road, too weary to heave himself up.

Then he heard or felt something give way underground, and all of his miner's instincts rose up in his throat. He had a vision of Cathedral Stope giving way, and a lot of rock shifting about underground, as in an earthquake. He thought he heard a rumble, and he was certain that he felt the bank tremble.

But no, it was all even more terrible and more urgent than that. The weight of water and debris overground was threatening the very bank on which he was clinging.

Shaun Mee, the blasphemer, started to pray. He remembered the Lord's Prayer and one or two hymns. He remembered the prayer for Camwul Community School, something about keeping your eye on the ball. And then, from somewhere deep underground, he heard the old men of Wheel Cuckoo singing as they tramped homewards towards the ladders:

"Lead kindly light, amid th'encircling gloom. Lead thou me on. The night is dark, and I am far from home, lead thou me on."

He thought he heard the young boys in the gold mines of Jo'burg, who said goodbye to their mother at the garden gate, who went out from the railway station at Camwul and did not return again:

"Keep thou my feet; I do not ask to see
The distant scene; one step enough for me."

After a while, he pulled himself together, and steeled himself to scramble along the embankment, above the muddy lake that was now rising steadily, threatening to pour over the surface of the road, taking him with it.

By a miracle, he got away from the lake that was pushing against the embankment, far enough to feel safe. Then he made a last effort and climbed up on to the tarmac. The rain was still falling, though it had lessened. Shaun Mee lay flat on the road for a while, no longer shivering or feeling cold at all, in fact he felt quite hot. He felt a kind of liberation, and wanted to throw off his clothes, but he thought somebody might see him naked on the road and think he was a dangerous nutter. After a while, he got to his knees, and then to his feet. It was all right up here on the road. He could see Dingo's caravan in the distance. He could almost wave to Dingo, but he had a feeling Dingo wasn't in. Anyway, Dingo's caravan was safe on that side of the road. It was a bit further up on the hillside, where the Irish road men had left it. It wasn't threatened by the torrent that was now just beginning to spill over the tarmac. In fact, he thought the road might be all right now that the lake was spilling over.

But then he saw a terrible brown wave, a wall of water and debris flooding down the valley, gouging out the Lannarth stream. In slow motion, it seemed to skate over the dammed up lake and flood down, banging rocks and even tree trunks onto the far side of the road, loosening the embankment on the far side. Mee felt the road tremble beneath him.

His instincts were to run away, but he was fascinated, and crept closer to the deluge. He knew the bank would collapse, but somehow, he thought the road would hold, even so. He stood on the trembling tarmac and thought, "This is crazy. This is not happening." Then he felt another long rumble, and saw the road slump down. He looked at his watch, but could not see the time, and still the maddening choir in his mind sang on, voices snatched away of a swelling chorus of all the mining men who had ever sung in the torrent and the gloom:

"I was not ever thus, nor prayed that thou... wouldst lead me on... I loved to choose my path, yet still somehow, lead thou me on. I loved the garish day, and in spite of fears, pride willed my soul... remember not past years..."

Who knows how long Shaun Mee stood there before the road collapsed in front of him with a great sigh and sailed on down to Maynard's Cove, to help Maynard's caravans on their way to the sea? From now on, everything passed in a dream before Shaun Mee's eyes. For a moment, in the gloom, he thought he saw Dingo emerge from his caravan on the safe side of the road and stand and point at the ground. Just for a while, Shaun Mee thought he saw, under the lake that was draining now more slowly into the valley, the footings and the foundations of Dingo's old scrap yard, of Dingo's old palace in the yard. He seemed to see it all revealed in slow motion, the foundations of Dingo's flimsy tar-barrel house and the sheds, the remains of cars and machinery that were part of Dingo's old place, all slipping away under the water and tumbling down the valley.

Certainly he saw a piece of concrete tear away from the bedrock and a solid wooden box burst open and spill out its contents. He saw them glint and gleam and a roaring voice in his ear laughed, *ching*, yes, yes, this was his lucky day after all. He had struck his gold. Dingo's Krugerrands began to tumble out and rest on the shallow, sandy bottom, where all seemed clear and calm. He took off his jacket and boots and crept forward, very slowly, onto the trembling, undermined, black crusted lip of tarmac. In the growling of the waters, he saw white-aproned children, boys and girls, tumbling out, chattering together, streaming out from low, straw roofed cottages. They cried to him not to turn back, not now, not when he was nearly all the way across to the gold fields, these fields of gold. The great choir swelled with clarity to the last, as he fixed his eyes on the yellow metal beneath the tide and sang out with all the mighty wind of the organ's bellows.

"And with the morn, those angel faces smile,
Which I have loved long since, and lost a while."

* * *

In Maynard's Cove, a strange thing was happening. Maynard's caravans were floating out of their field, smashing and climbing through and over the wall like big demented sheep, down the river, round the bend and bobbing into the sea. Hetty Pengelly, sitting in her window on Eastcliff, thought it was most peculiar. She had never seen the like. Using all of her binoculars, she saw that the small lobster fleet was on its way back for tea. She started waving, but of course it was useless. Her cries could not be heard beyond her hermetically sealed, weather proofed, tripleglazed lounge windows, which were leaking, leaving large pools of water on the window ledges and carpets.

Hetty went into the kitchen for a cup of tea and thought, Gar, this was really terrible, with bits of scoria, earth and deads moving down the cliffs. It was like

Aberfan. Her palm tree had fallen over and the daffodils looked as though they were trying to bury themselves under the mud in the garden. Patches were forming and dripping in a corner of the kitchen. She heard the toilet downstairs bubbling and gurgling. Then the sink started. Ought she to ring somebody? No, it was well drained, up here. Then she thought, well, everybody would be in the same boat, so it was best to sit it out. Her neighbours, what neighbours she had, seemed to be sitting it out. Everybody was indoors. The rain was bound to stop sometime. Out of the back window, she saw a lump of stone fall off one of the done-up heritage mine chimneys and crash down into a shaft, taking the health and safety shaft-capping cone with it. Oh well. There'd been no need to do up an old engine house in the first place: she didn't believe in it. Even the black and brown rats were moving down the cliff towards the harbour, where there were dry holds in the coasters.

After an hour, the rain seemed to abate a little bit, and she composed herself, combed her iron grey hair and went back into the chilly, damp lounge. The night storage heaters had come on, which steamed up the windows. She fetched a dry cloth and went to clean the glass.

It was then that she noticed that the Pengos lobster fleet had come out and had joined the Maynard Cove fleet at the brown water line, where the caravans and the cars and now the big freezers from the tourist cafes were floating about in the ocean. Unbelievable. They couldn't stand each other. They was always fighting and killing each other, they men. They'd got in each other's way for hundreds of years. What were they doing? They seemed to be working together, buzzing around, going back and forth, back and forth. You'd think they was foraging or harvesting or something, only it was all arbitrary, there was no method to it. It was as though they were excited and were picking and plucking things up and out of the brown, turbid sea.

* * *

Christice had had enough of the rain. There was nothing on the radio except some sort of afternoon play about a flood that went on and on and on without any proper plot or conclusion. She was sick of it and turned it off. The television didn't work, for some reason, so she sat about in bed for a while, reading a novel about a fisherman. All the rain outside made her feel chilly, so she found a bottle of something in a drawer and had a drink. Then she turned over and tried to go to sleep, but found it difficult.

Finally, at the end of a long afternoon, she tried to turn on the light. It didn't work, so she opened the curtains.

Imagine her surprise and fury when she saw that a damp patch was forming over the wardrobe.

She telephoned the estate manager on his mobile telephone.

"Would you send two men up immediately to move a wardrobe, Mr Cruise? Either someone has left a window open in the Schoolroom above, or the rain is coming in through the roof again." What a ghastly, hopeless house. She hated it.

* * *

Chapter Fourteen

And I will lay my vengeance upon Edom

Ezekiel 25:14

Tuesday April the eighteenth

Morning broke over a dank landscape. The blackened heather and gorse steamed in the warming sun. Curtains opened just a little and then closed quickly once more. It was anounced on the radio that only one inhabitant in all the parish failed to survive, and that was Shaun Mee. He was one of the few who were swept out to sea, though nobody could quite understand how or why. He couldn't tell them, because he never survived the helicopter ride to the hospital. Pirate Radio said he died of exposure. People laughed and said, that was the Mees all over.

By lunchtime, the Steam Engine was filled with people chatting amicably: unusually amicably, in fact. They seemed to be having a laugh about Maynard's caravans and cars floating past Levy Point as far as the cardinal buoy, before smashing in again and bringing with them a great harvest of insurance payouts. They were not so pleased about the parish warehouse being depleted, and it was agreed that without another wreck, there could be hard times ahead; but they were all in it together, and even the men of Pengos, who had mounted a tremendous salvage operation in the dark, were spoken of in generous and friendly terms.

The evening saw whole families scrabbling about on the sands, picking up little packets and smoking themselves silly on dried-out weed. Some of the kids slid and fell off the cliffs onto the rocks or into the open-air bathing pool, but nobody seemed to get hurt. For a few days, the whole parish seemed to be living in some sort of fool's paradise, even taking their camping gear down to the beach, catching bass to stave off hunger and forgetting all about work.

It was said that up at the Big House, things were grim. Mr Gwarior went about with a black expression and Bodruggan had gone off his tobacco entirely. Bodruggan practically boarded himself up in his folly, his gardening tools and wheelbarrow cleaned up and leaning against the wall. Estate workers' wives whispered that when Shaun Mee was plucked half dead out of the sea, he was still clutching a gold coin or a Pot of Gold token that he had somehow picked up out of the tons of mud that poured down the cliffs, off the fields, down the drains, through the adits and into Maynard's Cove, during the flood. But no-one knew how that could have come about: unless the solitary gold coin was one of Dingo's lost hoard of Krugerrands. And that was possible, because Dingo had that traphatch under his land somewhere, that was covered up by the new by-pass that got ripped up in the flood. And it was a known fact that Dingo spent the winter in his caravan, just staring and glaring out at the new road. So the Krugerrands must have been there. Then again, Dingo had not been seen for a day or two, though the caravan was intact. Dingo was keeping his head down. Perhaps he'd found his coins again, when the road was ripped up. Everybody hoped so, because that would be justice done. And justice was what everybody was after in the end, wasn' them?

* * *

"Go, my son. And sin no more." Dingo was woken up by a voice that was his own, and yet it was no voice of his. He sat up, banging his head on the orange box above his narrow bunk. He leaned on his elbow and listened to the black night that filled the caravan. It was a voice of infinite sorrow, and yet of unaccountable command. It wanted no answer. It filled the world with its agony and with its lonely resolution. Dingo slipped out of his blankets and went outside. The woods were lovely, dark and deep. There was no traffic on the devastated road, no sound. For help, Dingo looked to the dense tree canopy and the empty sky beyond, where the graying, pockmarked moon had all but burnt itself out. He saw a star fall, and thought of Icarus, and of the boy's spirit rising from out of the sea, up to the heavens, to play with the stars. The rain was over, the flood was down. The people were still asleep. He knew that now was the time.

In the blackness, Dingo dug up the Unemployment Benefit money that he had buried in the tin box he bought from the charity shop in Camwul. In the pre-dawn, Dingo left the caravan in the woods. He left his wire compound open and he left his caravan door unlocked, because he hated to see locks broken. He wore his one sharp suit, the suit he wore the day they convicted him; the suit he wore twelve years later, when he walked away from the prison gates. He wore the leather shoes he wore then, with the old-fashioned toes.

Now a fitter, leaner man, he slipped away through the woods in the dark, across the moors, climbing steadily until he came upon the Playing Place.

In the long shadow of the Steam Engine lights, Dingo took one last look at the Coen Finger longstone, placing his cheek upon it and swearing a final oath of renunciation. Then, wiping all traces of the stone's yellow lichen from his face, he crossed the dark iron-age Round to the back of the Steam Engine pub, where he once held court in a back room and played cards and brooded over the face of Christice Gwarior and brooded over the fate of his son, Wally, until it all got out of proportion in his mind and he named Wally's killer, though he had no evidence, but vengeance is mine, saith the Lord, not his, not Dingo's. Dodging the security lights, he crossed to the looming twin houses of Montana and Mexico, Carlyon houses, where, as a young man, as no-good Dingo, he had spied on Christice Gruzelier through a thick privet hedge, the unreachable, the unattainable. But he'd had her; he'd had her finally, when he was in his prime, when by legend he was the richest man in all Cornwall, and it came to no good. It bore bitter fruit in the dark, without his knowledge, and it led to this. This revelation. Too late. Too late. He crossed again to the vicarage and the Parish

Church of St Coen, where, as a wealthy man, he had been a respectable Church Warden, whose job it was to count the hymn books and receive his blessing. God knows, he had need of a blessing. In the churchyard, in the darkness, not knowing that a grave was there, he crossed Robin Cookson's unmarked mound. Standing on the curbstone of Ambrose the sailor's grave, he traced the letters on his father's elaborate headstone: Seamus Dingle of Sligo Bay. A lie. A rich man's lie, a monument to Dingo's own vanity. Stuck up there when Dingo had money and cherished respectability. As though his rotten, sly father had been a noble fisherman. Well, it was a lie. And there, amongst the modest dead, Alfred Gruzelier's neglected granite headstone, nearly overgrown with ivy, leaning in the clay already. Jake's grandfathers, whom Jake would never know, side by side, by some weird and ghastly chance. How many more? How many more young men grew up and went through life not knowing their true lineage? How many more in this lie of a churchyard and this dirty lie of a parish record? Why did he not say anything to the boy? Why did he not tell the boy, when he had his one opportunity: "It is I: I am your father, not him, not the ponce, Gwarior, but I, Dingo the tramp?" Why? Because Bodruggan was there and the boy was so innocent, in his riding coat and his big riding boots, the young squire of Carlyon. You couldn't destroy that. And the next time he saw him, he was smiling and dreaming behind the security bars of Henry Gwarior's office, in Carlyon, where he belonged with his mother. Nothing could be done to change the way things were. Nor should it. No man should put asunder Henry and Christice Gwarior and their son and heir. No man should be instrumental in shattering this great illusion, or in tearing this silk veil, this Patronymia. He had believed in the legend of Carlyon, that the Gwariors would leave and the Carlyons would return: but he had not thought when he first entered the great house that his blood would be the blood that usurped the Gwariors. He did not want this burden. He was unworthy of it.

Did it matter in the end? Did any of it matter that Jake would not know? That Jake's mother would die with the secret, if her luck held; and Jake's own father would never be known to him? No, it didn't matter in the end. His blood would live, and her blood would live in Carlyon. Why should he not be happy in this? His blood would rule Carlyon for all the generations afterwards. Wouldn't his own father have wanted that? Been proud of that? There was nothing Dingo should do now, except to steal away, to go away and swear to stay away, or a greater storm would drown them all. He had already hesitated too long. Arthur Bodruggan was right.

Yet where was the triumph of blood? He could not feel it.

And walking the Round one last time, his light footsteps sounding and resounding again, as though to contain him and cover him and protect him in this perpetual motion of walking, he swore again his final oath of renunciation. He would not: he would not... yet, swearing his final oath, he could not say amen. Was he in the wrong to go? Should he stay after all? Wait in the dark for the boy to find out? He would not. It would raise uncontrollable forces. It would ruin her and the boy. Where could he put them, when they were found out? In Irene's council house in Keen? Why could he not say amen?

But he would let the cunt Henry Gwarior be the father of Jake Gwarior. For he, Dingo, could not be his father. This was his judgment. To lose his own son. And then to lose another. To see another son blossom and bloom and go to the bad too early. Too early. Without knowing his own father. Because Dingo killed somebody else's son. For which, a twelve year stretch was nothing at all. The loss of his status was nothing. The loss of the woman who sat like a stuffed gin-soaked prune in the upstairs window in the great crumbling house, saying nothing. Unreachable. Unshakable. Useless to his already suffering son. The loss of his yard. The loss of his Krugerrands. His gold. His boat. His caravan. He'd ended up with worse than nothing in St Coen. Nothing had come of nothing of nothing.

Amos Dingle stopped walking. He found himself beside the Coen longstone in the middle of the Round, the great wide ancient playing-place of the tea-treat, the wrestling match and the mystery and the miracle play; and he heard them in the round, the actors and the players and the filthy, the sore and the sacrificed. This was the darkest moment, when the flimsy veiled dwellings of man melted away and only the stones rose and became silent silent suffering crowds of watchers in the bat bible crow blackness of night: to judge him, Amos Dingle.

213

Because the man was mortally afraid in that moment, he shut his eyes and kissed the spinning stone, and held on to the stone, unthinking; and the spinning stone was an unmoving presence until the stone seemed to hum and hum in the darkness as it reached for the sun, "Amen Amos, I am... "

And somewhere high above the Round, a solitary lark burst out, streaming out with ribbons of sound.

And the churchyard trees stirred with the wake-up clatter of rooks.

And the sparrows rose up to settle and sob in the high privet hedges of Mexico and Montana houses.

And wild dog that he was, he slipped away, just as the sun slid up and lit the St Coen longstone, old Dingo slipped down across Ting Tang and the tinners' moors into the valley of shadow to Camwul unseen: to the up line of Brunel's old western railway, where he crossed the derelict broccoli and daffodil goods yard, he stepped onto the early morning milk train, whilst the sorters were shouting and whistling and pushing the post bags into the mail vans.

* * *

Books in the same series by Myrna Combellack

The Playing Place: a Cornish Round

A Fine Place: the Cornish Estate

Other books by Myrna Combellack

The Permanent History of Penaluna's Van

Cuts in the Face: stories from Cornwall

The Mistress of Grammar

The Camborne Play: a verse translation of *Beunans Meriasek*

If you liked this book (or if you didn't) contact the author at Salisbury@Freenet.co.uk